"I wonder what you're afte

A drink? Conversation? Or something more?" Isabel sat forward and drew her finger around the rim of her glass, looking at him, unafraid to confront him with her gaze.

"I want whatever you might be willing to give me," he admitted.

She smiled and the slightest blush crossed her cheeks. Good God, she was so beautiful he had to wonder if he was dreaming. "So I'm in the driver's seat. That's what you're telling me."

"Of course. As it should be, right?"

She nodded, arching her eyebrows in a way that suggested she hadn't quite been prepared for where their conversation had turned. He loved feeling like he could surprise her, even if the boost to his ego might be completely unwarranted.

"So, Jeremy. Since I'm in charge, let me just share one more thing about myself. I don't know how you feel about good views, but I have a spectacular one of the city. Upstairs in my room."

* * *

A Christmas Rendezvous concludes
the Eden Empire series.

Dear Reader,

Thanks for picking up *A Christmas Rendezvous*! I'm a bit sad that it's time for the travails of the Eden family to wrap up, but I'm sure that if you've been reading all along, you're dying to know what happens. And if this is your first in the series, don't be afraid to jump right in.

There's a bit of a shift in this story, as the heroine is not a member of the Eden family, but rather attorney Isabel, Sam Blackwell's sister. Eden's department store is under siege, and I liked the idea of someone from the outside coming in to help the sisters fight this battle. Unfortunately for Isabel, her primary opponent in this legal war is Jeremy, the guy she had a one-night stand with a week before she took on the case. Talk about an "oops" moment.

Isabel and Jeremy each have their own obstacles when it comes to love, but one thing I explored in this book is what it's like when time becomes one of those hurdles. Isabel is thirty-eight and Jeremy is forty, and they both want to get on with their lives and find happiness with someone they love. Whether love is found young or old or you're still looking, I think that's a very relatable feeling.

I sincerely hope you enjoyed the Eden Empire series. I have loved writing every book. Drop me a line anytime at karen@karenbooth.net. I love hearing from readers!

Karen

KAREN BOOTH

A CHRISTMAS RENDEZVOUS

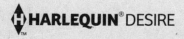

Recycling programs
for this product may
not exist in your area.

ISBN-13: 978-1-335-60400-2

A Christmas Rendezvous

Printed in U.S.A.

Karen Booth is a Midwestern girl transplanted in the South, raised on '80s music and repeated readings of *Forever* by Judy Blume. When she takes a break from the art of romance, she's listening to music with her nearly grown kids or sweet-talking her husband into making her a cocktail. Learn more about Karen at karenbooth.net.

Books by Karen Booth

Harlequin Desire

The Best Man's Baby
The Ten-Day Baby Takeover
Snowed in with a Billionaire

The Eden Empire

A Christmas Temptation
A Cinderella Seduction
A Bet with Benefits
A Christmas Seduction
A Christmas Rendezvous

Dynasties: Secrets of the A-List

Tempted by Scandal

Visit her Author Profile page at Harlequin.com, or karenbooth.net, for more titles.

You can find Karen Booth on Facebook, along with other Harlequin Desire authors, at Facebook.com/harlequindesireauthors!

For Val Skorup. You are the best cheerleader a person could ever want, a great friend and a total rock star.

One

Isabel Blackwell's head had hardly hit the pillow when the hotel alarm went off. The fire alarm.

Frustrated and annoyed, she sat up in bed and shoved back her sleep mask while the siren droned on out in the hall. This was getting old. The luxury Bacharach New York hotel had been her home for nearly two weeks and this was the fourth time the fire alarm had sounded. She'd intentionally gone to bed early to try to sleep away her difficult day. Her brother, Sam, had convinced her to take on a legal case she did not want—saving Eden's Department Store from a man with a vendetta and a decades-old promissory note. So much for the escape of a good night's rest.

"Attention, guests," the prerecorded message sounded over the hallway PA system. "Please proceed to the nearest fire exit in an orderly manner. Do not use the elevators. I repeat, do not use the elevators. Thank you."

"Do *not* use the elevators," Isabel mumbled to herself in a robotic voice. She tossed back the comforter, grabbed her robe, shoved her feet into a pair of ballet flats and dutifully shuffled down the hallway with the other guests. It was not quite 10:00 p.m., so she was the only one in her pajamas, but she refused to be embarrassed by it. Hers were pale pink silk charmeuse and she'd spent a fortune on them. Plus, if anyone should be feeling self-conscious, it was the hotel management. They needed to get their property under control.

She followed along down the stairs, through the lobby past the befuddled and apologetic bell captain, and out onto the street. Early December was not an ideal time to be parading around a Manhattan sidewalk in silk pj's, but she hoped that by now, the hotel staff had finely honed their skills of determining whether there was an actual fire.

The manager shot out of the revolving door, frantic. "Folks, I am so sorry. We're working as fast as we can to get you back inside and to your rooms." He fished a stack of cards from his suit pocket and began doling them out. "Please. Everyone. Enjoy a complimentary cocktail at the bar as our way of apologizing."

Isabel took his offering. She wasn't about to pass up a free drink.

"What if you already have one waiting for you?" a low rumble of a voice behind her muttered.

Isabel turned and her jaw went slack. Standing before her was a vision so handsome she found herself wondering if she had actually fallen asleep upstairs and was now in the middle of a splendidly hot dream. Tall and trim, the voice had a strong square jaw covered in neatly trimmed scruff, steely gray eyes and extremely enticing bedhead hair. It had even gone a very sexy salt-and-pepper at the temples, pure kryptonite for Isabel. She had a real weakness for a distinguished man. "You had to leave a drink behind?" she had the presence of mind to ask. "That's a very sad story."

The voice crossed his arms and looked off through the hotel's glass doors, longingly. "The bartender had just poured the best Manhattan I've ever had. And it's wasting away in there." He then returned his sights to her, his vision drifting down to her feet, then lazily winding its way back up. As he took in every inch of her, it warmed her from head to toe. "Aren't you freezing?"

"No." She shook her head. "I run hot."

A corner of his mouth curled in amusement, and that was when she noticed exactly how scrumptious his lips were. He offered his hand. "Jeremy."

"Isabel." She wrapped her fingers around his, and found herself frozen in place. He wasn't moving, either. No, they were both holding on, heat and a steady current coursing between them. It had been too long since she'd shared even an instant of flirtation with a man, let alone a chemistry-laden minute or two. Her job was always getting in the way, a big reason she disliked it so much.

"You weren't kidding," he said. "How are you so warm?"

How are you so hot? "Lucky, I guess."

"Ladies and gentlemen," the hotel manager announced, poking his head out of the door. "Turns out it was a false alarm. You may go back inside."

"Looks like you can go rescue your Manhattan," Isabel said to Jeremy.

"Join me? I hate to drink alone." He cocked his head to one side and both eyebrows popped up in invitation.

Isabel had been fully prepared to go back upstairs and simply take a few thoughts of dreamy Jeremy for a spin as she drifted off to sleep. "I'm in my pajamas."

"Don't forget the sleep mask." He reached up and plucked it from her hair. "Do these things really work?"

She smoothed back her hair, deciding this was only a good sign—he'd invited her to have a drink with him when she looked far less than her best. "They do work. Once you get used to it."

"I've never tried one. Maybe I should. I don't sleep that well."

Isabel fought back what she really wanted to say—that she wouldn't mind having the chance to make him slumber like a baby. Instead, she took the mask from his hand and tucked it into the pocket of her robe. "If you can stand to be seen with me, I'd love a drink."

"You could be wearing a potato sack and I'd still invite you for a drink." He stepped aside and with a flourish of his hand, invited her to lead the way.

Oh, Jeremy was smooth. For a moment she wondered if he was too much so. In her experience, men like that were only interested in fun. She'd moved to New York for a fresh start, so she could pursue a less unsavory line of legal work—adoption law, to be specific—and finally get serious about love. At thirty-eight, she was eager to get on with her life. Still, it was silly to judge yummy Jeremy by a few words in their first conversation. "Good to know your standards." Isabel marched inside and crossed the lobby, stopping at the bar entrance. Despite the generous disbursement of drink coupons from the manager, the room was sparsely occupied, with only a few people seated at the long mahogany bar. It was an elegant space, albeit a bit stuck in time, with black-and-white-checkerboard floors and crystal chandeliers dripping from the barrel ceiling. "You'll have to let me know where you left your drink behind."

"Over here." Jeremy strolled ahead and Isabel took her chance to watch him from behind. The view was stunning—a sharp shoulder line atop a towering lean frame. His midnight-blue suit jacket obscured his backside, but she could imagine how spectacular it must be. He arrived at a corner table, and sure enough, there was his drink, along with a stack of papers, which he quickly shuffled into a briefcase.

"You really did leave in a hurry," she said. "Is this your first night staying here? I don't take the fire alarm all that seriously anymore. Most of the time it's nothing."

"I'm not a guest. I just had a meeting. I actually live in Brooklyn, but I thought I'd grab a drink before I headed home." He slid her a sly look. "Now I'm glad I did."

Isabel knew she should ask what he did for a living, but that would only lead to discussion of her own occupation. The last thing she wanted to do was talk about being a lawyer, a career she'd once dreamed of but that had since turned into a bit of a nightmare, another reason for moving away from Washington, DC. She'd somehow gone from earnest attorney to a political "fixer," cleaning up the personal messes of the powerful. She was good at it. Very good, actually. But she'd grown weary of that particular rat race. And in Washington, everyone was a rodent of one form or another.

"What would you like to drink?" Jeremy asked, pulling out a chair for her.

Isabel eased into the seat, which was sumptuously upholstered in white velvet with black trim.

"I'll have a gin and tonic, two limes." She reached into her robe and pulled out the drink coupon, holding it out for Jeremy.

"Save that for a rainy day. It was my invitation. I intend to buy you a drink."

Isabel had to smile. It'd been a long time since a man had treated her nicely and actually made an effort. She'd been starting to wonder if gentlemanly behavior was a lost art. "Thank you."

Jeremy flagged down the bartender and was back with her drink in a few minutes. He sat next to her, his warm scent settling over her. It was both woodsy and citrusy, conjuring visions of a romantic fire crackling away. "So, tell me about yourself. What do you do?"

She had to make a choice right then and there as to how this night was going to go. Either they would do the same old getting-to-know-you routine that every man and woman who have just met must seemingly pursue, or they would head in a different direction. Coming to New York was supposed to be a fresh start for Isabel and she intended to follow through on that. She would not cling to old habits. She would try something new.

She reached out and set her hand on Jeremy's, which was resting on the tabletop. "I vote that we don't talk about work. At all. I don't think we should talk about where we went to school or who we used to date or how many important people we know."

Jeremy's eyes darkened, but there was a spark

behind them—a mischievous glint. He was, at the very least, intrigued. "Okay, then. What do you want to talk about?"

She stirred her drink, not letting go of his hand. She loved that they already had this unspoken familiarity. Like they understood each other, and so soon after meeting each other. "I don't know. A little brutal honesty between strangers?"

He laughed and turned his hand until their palms were flat against each other. He clasped his fingers around hers. How that one touch could convey so much, she wasn't sure, but excitement bubbled up inside her so fast she thought she might pop like a cork from a champagne bottle. It was as if she'd been in a deep sleep and her entire body had rattled back to life. She wasn't the sort of woman who pinned a lot of hope on a man, but she found herself wondering where this might go.

"Like truth or dare, but just the truth part?" he asked.

Isabel swallowed hard, but did her best to convey cool. "Oh, no. I never said I wasn't up for a dare."

Jeremy was so tempted to dare Isabel to kiss him, he had to issue himself a mental warning: *Slow down, buddy.* He was essentially fearless, but he wasn't the guy to make leaps with a woman. Not anymore. He greatly enjoyed their company, but he'd been burned badly by a toxic marriage and the hellish divorce that followed. Since then, he'd learned to employ caution, but he did occasionally need to remind himself.

Still, he didn't want to waste his evening ruminating on his past mistakes. Not now. Not when he was sitting with Isabel, a woman who made him want to employ zero restraint. She was not only a captivating beauty, with sleek black hair framing a flawless complexion and warm brown eyes; she had a demeanor unlike any he'd ever encountered, from anyone—man or woman. What person goes to a bar in pale pink silk pajamas and matching robe and seems wholly comfortable? And the bit about not trying to impress each other? That was like a breath of fresh air. If he had to start talking about his job, he'd just get stressed. Especially after the meeting he'd had in this very bar an hour ago.

"I'm afraid I haven't played truth or dare since I was a teenager," he admitted.

"Me, neither. And almost all of the dares seemed to involve kissing."

It was as if she'd read his mind.

"But we aren't teenagers anymore, are we?" she added.

"Not me. I turned forty this year." Jeremy cleared his throat, struggling to keep up with her. He was usually laser-focused on a retort. As a lawyer, he got plenty of practice. "Okay, then. Tell me something almost nobody knows about you."

She smiled cleverly, stirring her drink. "That could take all night. I have lots of secrets." She bent her neck to one side and absentmindedly traced her delicate fingers along her collarbone.

The first secret Jeremy wanted to know was what was under those pajamas. He wanted to know *who* was under there—what Isabel would kiss like. What her touch would be like, what it would be like to have her naked form pressed against his. "How about three things I need to know about you? As a person. Three things you believe in."

She twisted up her beautiful lips, seeming deep in thought. "Okay. I believe that there is no good reason to lie, but that doesn't mean you have to confess everything. I believe that a good nap will cure most problems. And I believe that love is ultimately the only thing that ever saves anyone."

"Really?" Jeremy found that last part a bit too sunny and optimistic, but then again, he had his reasons for rolling his eyes at love.

"Like I said, a little brutal honesty between strangers. I have no reason to be anything less than ridiculously open and bare my soul."

"You're a therapist, aren't you? One of those people you pay hundreds of dollars an hour to, just so you can reveal the most humiliating things you've ever done."

She shook her head. "Hey. That's against the rules. We said we weren't going to talk about work."

"So I'm right. You *are* a therapist."

"No, you aren't right." She flashed her wide, warm eyes at him. "You aren't wrong, either."

Jeremy had to laugh while he marveled at the puzzle of Isabel. He wanted to peel back her layers, one by one… He suspected there were a lot of surprises to be found. "I suppose you want me to tell you my three truths now, huh?"

"It's only fair."

He had to think for a moment, knowing he had to match the clever balance she'd struck between revealing all and piquing his interest. He would not allow himself to be completely outdone by Isabel. "I believe that taking yourself too seriously is a trap. I believe that apologizing for making a lot of money is stupid. And I believe that there's nothing wrong with having fun."

She nodded, seemingly digesting his words. "Those are all very interesting."

"You're definitely a therapist."

"And you are definitely not good at following rules."

He shrugged. "Most rules are arbitrary."

"Like what?"

"Like the one that says you shouldn't invite a woman wearing her pajamas on a New York City sidewalk out for a drink."

She pointed her finger at him. "Yes. You're so right. That is a stupid rule."

He downed the last of his drink, sensing this was the moment when he had to decide whether he wanted to angle for an invitation upstairs. Fear was a big factor. He didn't want to endure a rejection from

Isabel. Something told him she could deliver one in a particularly devastating way. "And yet I went there, didn't I? I took the chance."

"Yes, you did, didn't you? Which makes me wonder what you're after, Jeremy. A drink? Conversation? Or something more?" Isabel sat forward and drew her finger around the rim of her glass, looking at him, unafraid to confront him with her gaze.

He had to break the spell she had him under, but when he let his sights wander, it only got worse. The front of her robe had gaped open, revealing the gentle curve of the top of one breast. Jeremy felt the heat rising in his body, starting in his belly and radiating outward, up to his chest and down to his thighs. It would be so easy to blame it on the drink, but that heat was all created by Isabel. She pulled it out of thin air with her pouty lips, with her dark and sultry eyes, and with her sharp conversational skills. He was not the type to ask for more. Asking for anything only made things messy. It put you at a disadvantage, and he hated not feeling as though he had every weapon imaginable at his disposal. What was it about Isabel that made him want to lie down and give her everything?

"I want whatever you might be willing to give me," he admitted.

She smiled and the faintest blush crossed her cheeks. Good God, she was so beautiful he had to wonder if all of this was really happening. "So I'm in the driver's seat. That's what you're telling me."

"Of course. As it should be, right?"

She nodded, arching her eyebrows in a way that suggested she hadn't quite been prepared for the way their conversation had turned. He loved feeling like he could surprise her, even if the boost to his ego might be completely unwarranted. "So, Jeremy. Since I'm in charge, let me just share one more thing about myself. I don't know how you feel about good views, but I have a spectacular one of the city. Upstairs in my room."

Jeremy felt as though Isabel had just rolled Christmas, his birthday and Super Bowl Sunday into one day. "Funny you should ask, because I am a huge fan of views." He leaned closer and lowered his head, his heart thundering away in his chest like a summer storm.

Isabel drifted closer to him until their noses were almost touching. The rest of the room had faded away. Other people and their surroundings were a distant thought. It was just the two of them, their breaths in sync and their intentions apparently aligned, as well. "Truth or dare," she whispered.

"Dare," he answered without hesitation.

"Good answer." Her lips met his in the slightest of kisses. Her mouth only teased him, softer and more supple than he'd dared to imagine. She angled her head and took the kiss deeper, grasping his shoulder and digging her nails into his jacket. Her lips parted and her tongue skated along his lower lip, making every testosterone-driven part of him switch into high gear. The blood was pumping so fast it was hard to know which way was up.

He reached for her hip, the silk of her robe impossibly cool and soft against his skin. He pulled her closer, clawing at the tie at her waist, needing her. Wanting her. Like he needed to breathe or eat or drink water. This whole business of not knowing much about each other was so hot. It left him wondering what the night had in store, when he hadn't been willing to gamble on the unknown in a long time.

"You never gave me my dare," he said, coming up for air.

"I dare you to come upstairs and take off your suit, Jeremy. I dare you to rock my world."

Two

It took every ounce of self-control Jeremy had to discreetly walk across that hotel lobby with Isabel. His gut was telling him to take her hand and run as fast as he could, jab the elevator button and get things going between them the instant they were inside. As long as they were alone.

Unfortunately, the elevator was not cooperating. "This thing is so slow," Isabel said, jamming the button a second time. She subtly leaned against him and rubbed the side of his thigh with her hand.

Everything in his body went so tight it felt as though he was strapped to a piece of wood. Blood drained from his hands and feet and rushed straight to the center of his body. He swallowed back a groan and strategically held his briefcase to obscure anyone's view of his crotch. His erection felt like it had its own pulse. He needed Isabel, now.

Finally the elevator dinged and they rushed on board as soon as the other passengers were off. He'd hoped they'd be able to ride alone, but at the last minute, someone shoved their hand between the doors.

It was an older gray-haired woman. "I'm sorry. Thought I'd catch it while I could. Otherwise you end up waiting forever."

"So true," Isabel said. She leaned against the back wall, standing right next to Jeremy. She looked over at him as her hand again caressed his thigh. She bit her lower lip and he thought he might faint. She was too hot for words.

Mercifully, the woman got off the elevator at the fifth floor, but being alone with Isabel only opened the floodgates. He dropped his briefcase as they smashed into each other, kissing hard, tongues and wet lips, insistent hands everywhere. He yanked at the tie on her robe, then fumbled with the buttons on her pajama top. Hers were inside his suit jacket, tugging his shirt out from the waist of his pants. By the time the elevator dinged on the eighteenth floor, they were both in a disheveled state of near-undress.

Isabel picked up his briefcase, handed it to him and dashed down the hall, with Jeremy in close pursuit. She pulled her key card from her robe pocket and Jeremy stole a look down the front of her pajama top, which was already half-unbuttoned. Her breasts were full, her skin creamy and he couldn't wait to have his hands all over them.

Isabel flung open the door and Jeremy again dropped his briefcase, relieved he didn't need to keep track of it anymore. Isabel took off her robe and undid the last two buttons on her pajama top, tossing it to the floor. He cupped her breasts in both hands, her skin even softer and more velvety smooth than he'd imagined. Her nipples tightened beneath his touch. He loved seeing and feeling how responsive she was to him. Her pajama pants hung loosely below her belly button, clinging to her curvy hips. He wanted to see every inch of her and with a single tug of the drawstring at her waist, they slumped to the floor. She had no panties on underneath and that view of everything to come made everything beneath his waist grow even tighter, even hotter.

"You have on way too many clothes," she said as she flew through the buttons on his shirt and he got rid of his jacket. She then seemed to notice exactly how fierce his erection was. "Very nice." She flattened her hand against the front of his pants and pressed hard, rubbing up and down firmly.

He wavered between full sight and blindness. It felt so impossibly good. He only wanted more. This time, Jeremy didn't have to disguise his reaction, and he let out a groan at full roar. Isabel responded by unzipping his pants while he toed off his shoes. A few seconds later, she had the rest of his clothes in a puddle on the floor. She wrapped her hand around his length and took careful strokes while he kissed her. It had been so long since he'd wanted a woman like he wanted her. Something about her left him letting down his guard.

"Do you have a condom?" he asked, realizing that he did not. This was not good planning on his part, but he did not make a regular habit of meeting women after work and going up to their hotel rooms.

"I do. In the bathroom. One minute." Isabel traipsed off and he watched her full bottom and long legs in graceful motion. He couldn't wait to be inside her.

She returned seconds later with a box, which she set on the bedside table after taking out a packet. She tore open the foil and closed in on him, a bit like a tiger stalks its prey. Jeremy liked feeling so wanted. It felt good to know that he still had the power to do this to a woman.

Isabel took the condom and gently placed it on the tip of his erection, then rolled it down his length, all while their gazes connected. She owned every touch, every action of her beautiful body, and Jeremy wanted to drown in her self-confidence. He wanted to live in the world she did—where there seemed to be zero reason to question oneself.

Across the room sat that big beautiful bed, with a crisp white comforter and countless pillows. But Jeremy wanted to make love to Isabel in every corner of this room, and the chair that was right next to him seemed like the perfect place to start. He took her hand and he sat down, easing his hips to the edge of the seat. Isabel didn't miss a beat, straddling his legs and placing her knees on the chair next to his hips. Jeremy reached between them and positioned himself, then Isabel lowered her body onto his. He kept both his hands on her hips while his sights were set solely on her stunning face. Her mouth went slack and she closed her eyes as she let him slide inside. She was a perfect fit. And Jeremy was nothing if not thankful to whatever forces in the universe had brought him to this moment.

Isabel dictated the pace, which was perfect for him. He wanted to know what she liked. Despite the fact that he had so much pent-up need inside him, this was all about her. He would not leave until she was fully satisfied. He eased one hand to her lower back and urged her to lean into him so he could kiss her. Fully and deeply. Meanwhile, Isabel rode his length up and down and Jeremy struggled to keep up, to keep from reaching his destination too soon. He did not want to disappoint her.

Their kisses were soft and wet, tongues sensuously twisting together. Jeremy caressed her breast with one hand while the other cupped her backside, his fingers curled into the soft and tender flesh. Isabel raked her hands through his hair over and over again, telling him with soft moans and subtle gasps that she was happy. He felt her tightening around him, and that matched her breaths, which had become ragged and torn.

"I'm close," she muttered into his ear, then kissed his neck.

He'd passed close several minutes ago and had since been skirting the edge, trying to ward off his climax. "Come for me."

Isabel planted her forehead against his and went for it, riding his length faster, sinking as far down as she could with every pass. Jeremy was fairly sure he had no blood flow to the rest of his body as he steeled himself. As soon as she let go and called out, he did the same, following behind her. Her muscles gathered around him tightly, over and over again, and the relief that washed over him was immense.

All he could think as the orgasm faded and Isabel collapsed against his chest was that he had to have her one more time. And quite possibly one more time after that.

"I need you again, Isabel." Jeremy smoothed his hand over her naked back and kissed her shoulder, bringing everything in her post-bliss body back to a quick simmer.

"Already?" she asked, slowly easing herself off his lap. She stepped over to the bed, where a mere hour or so ago she'd been attempting to sleep, and pulled back the comforter. She certainly hadn't thought at that time that she'd end up with a man in her room later.

"I'm going to need a minute or two, but I swear that's all." Jeremy padded off to the bathroom.

Isabel climbed into bed and immediately rested her head back on the pillow, staring up at the ceiling. *Wow.* She was glad Jeremy wanted more. That first time had been so hurried. She wanted the opportunity to savor him.

Moments later, he joined her, climbing in next to her and pressing his long body against hers. "You're incredible. Once was not enough."

She could already feel his erection against her leg. She was nothing if not impressed. Jeremy with the salt-and-pepper hair had a very quick recovery time. Of course she was on board. Considering that they hardly knew each other, he had an uncanny ability to hit all of her most sensitive spots. She really appreciated a man who picked up on her cues and followed suit.

"We need another condom," she said, kissing him deeply.

He rolled over and sat on the edge of the bed, took one from the box on the nightstand. Isabel turned to her side and swished her hand across the silky sheets, feeling his body heat still there. She admired his muscled back in the soft light from the window. He was in unbelievable shape and she was happy to reap the rewards.

When he turned back to her, he smiled. "You are so beautiful. I'm still trying to figure out how I managed to talk you into taking me upstairs."

She swatted his arm, then pulled him closer as he reclined next to her. "You're no slouch. Believe me."

He kissed her sweetly, then his approach turned more seductive, as he opened his mouth and their tongues found each other, swirling and swooping. He was an amazing kisser, there was no doubt about that. Isabel could have kissed him forever; they were in perfect sync. He rolled her to her back and hovered above her, holding his body weight with his firm arms. Isabel ran her hands from his wrists to his shoulders, her eyes closing and opening as he lowered his mouth to her neck, then her breast, taking her nipple between his lips. He was unhurried now, a stark contrast to the frenzied first time.

He positioned himself at her entrance and drove inside slowly, pushing her patience, letting her feel every inch as he filled her perfectly. Isabel rolled her head from side to side, feeling the cool pillow on her cheeks as Jeremy made the rest of her body red hot. She raised her knees to let him in deeper, and he was taking mind-bending strokes just like he had the first time. This was the advantage of a man later in life. He knew what he was doing.

He slipped his hand between their bodies and pressed his thumb against her apex, rolling in firm circles as he kept his even pace. She was surprised how quickly the tension wrapped itself around her, the way he drove her toward the edge of the cliff so perfectly. Right there. The climax was toying with her now, ebbing closer, then pulling away. Each pass brought it nearer and she could feel ahead of time just how intense it was going to be. She heard her own hums and moans, but her consciousness was so deep inside her own body that it came out muffled and fuzzy. Meanwhile, she became fitful and greedy, needing him closer. Needing more. She dug her heels into his backside, pulling him into her, and that was when the orgasm slammed into her, even harder and more intense than last time. This was an order of magnitude she hadn't been prepared for—sheer gratification awash in beautiful colors and hazy, un-worried thoughts.

As she became more aware of the here and now, Isabel could tell that Jeremy was also near his peak. His breaths were labored, but light, just like they had been the first time. Puffs of air that seemed to go in one direction. Just in. And further in. In one sudden movement, he jerked, then his torso froze in place, his hips flush against her bottom. She wrapped her legs around him tightly and raked her fingers up and down his strong back, feeling every defined muscle. As her own pleasure continued to swirl around her, she blazed a trail of hot kisses against his neck, want-ing to show her appreciation. Jeremy was magnifi-cent. Absolutely perfect.

"Oh, no," he groaned. "The condom. It broke."

Just like that, the spell was broken. "Did you?" she asked. Had she really just been thinking that this was perfect? She should have known better. That did not exist. Not for her, at least.

"Did I come? Yes." He rolled off of her and jumped up from the bed, rushing off to the bathroom.

Isabel closed her eyes and pinched her nose. *Great*. So much for her fun with handsome Jeremy. So much for the idea of a third time. Or a fourth. This was about to come to a quick end, she guessed, at least judging by how quickly he had retreated to the bathroom.

He returned a few seconds later with a towel wrapped around his waist. He paced, running his hands through his hair. "I don't know what to say, other than I'm sorry."

Her instinct was to make him feel better, even when she was feeling worse by the second. "Not your fault. It happens."

Awkward silence followed, and she knew that Jeremy was planning his escape. He had his lips pressed tightly together like he couldn't figure out what to do next. Part of her was tempted to point to the door and save them both the embarrassment. Part of her wanted to put on her sleep mask and convince herself this part wasn't happening. They'd had such an amazing night together. It didn't seem fair that it should end like this. But that was life. Nothing to do about it but move on.

He sat on the edge of the bed, but it was about as far away from her as possible. The divide between them now felt like it was a mile wide. In some ways, she felt like she knew him even less now than she had when they'd first met downstairs. "I don't even know your last name. What if I just got you pregnant?"

Isabel knew that uncertain edge in his voice. She'd

heard it before. One time in particular had been so painful she thought she might never recover. That had been over an actual pregnancy, not merely a fear of obligation. Her initial impression of Jeremy had been correct. He came off as smooth for a reason—he was all about the pursuit, not about sticking around. And that was fine. No harm, no foul. They hardly knew each other. It was understandable that he might feel trapped. It was now her job to let him off the hook, if only to allow herself to get on her with her life.

"If it makes you feel any better, my name is Isabel Blackwell."

He glanced over at her. "Oh. Okay. My last name is Sharp."

Isabel grabbed the sheet and pulled it up over herself. Exchanging last names had done nothing to make this situation more comfortable. If anything, it made it so much more obvious that she wasn't built for one-night stands.

Isabel scooted up in bed until her back was against the headboard. "Look. Don't worry about it. It's okay. I keep track of my cycle pretty closely. I don't think there's any chance we're in trouble." She'd under-sold that part by quite a bit. She'd been methodically tracking her periods for the last several years. If she managed to meet Mr. Right, she wanted to be able to try for a baby as soon as possible. Isabel prepared for everything in life. It was the best way to avoid surprises and the perfect distraction when you felt like the things you wanted weren't happening fast enough.

"Okay. Well, I wasn't sure if you wanted me to stay…" His voice trailed off, leaving Isabel to make the final declaration.

"No, Jeremy. It's okay. I think it's probably best at this point if you head home. I have a big meeting tomorrow and I'm sure you have things you need to do tomorrow. We probably both need a good night's sleep."

He nodded. "Sure. Yes. Of course." He got up from the bed and began collecting his clothes from their various locales across the room. He let go of the towel so he could step into his boxers, giving Isabel one last parting glance at perfect Jeremy. *Damn.* If only this hadn't started so absurdly. If only it hadn't ended so uncomfortably. He might have been a guy she would have wanted around for a while.

Wrapped up in the sheet, she climbed out of bed and padded past him to the bathroom. She quietly closed the door behind her and sucked in several deep breaths. *You're okay.* Moving to New York was supposed to be her new beginning, especially with men and the notion of having a personal life. So she'd had a false start. Jeremy was ultimately a nice guy. He was handsome, sexy and kind. They'd had some rotten luck, but that happened every day. Isabel needed to get past the idea that her fresh start was ruined by one mishap.

She stepped to the sink, took a sip of water from the

glass on the vanity and prepared herself to walk back out into the room. "Worse things have happened." When she opened the bathroom door, Jeremy was standing right outside, suit on but no tie. His briefcase was in his hand. For a moment, she wondered what he did for work. Probably a Wall Street guy. He seemed the type—cocky, good-looking, sure of himself. She wouldn't ask him now.

"Okay, then. You off?" she asked.

He nodded. "Yes. Thank you for tonight. It was really nice. I swear."

She had to laugh at what a sad and funny situation she'd gotten herself into. She stepped closer to him and stole one last kiss. "Jeremy. You were amazing. And I hope you have a lifetime of making money and finding fun wherever you go."

He smiled, but it wasn't a full-throttle grin, not the smile that had first sparked her curiosity or the chemistry between them. "I hope you find everything you're looking for, Isabel Blackwell."

With that, she opened the door and watched as he walked down the hall to the elevator. She hoped Jeremy was right. She didn't want to go too much longer waiting.

Three

Jeremy finally gave in at 4:37 a.m. His night's sleep was a lost cause. He climbed out from under his down comforter and sat on the edge of his bed, elbows on his knees, and ran a hand through his hair. A deep sigh escaped his lips, but he could have sworn he heard a word in it. A name. Isabel. *What the hell was that? What the hell happened?*

He'd never had a woman work her way into his psyche in such a short amount of time—mere hours. Sure, part of it was the fact that he was still stinging from the way he'd had to exit her room, and her life. When they'd been down at the bar flirting and she offered the invitation to come upstairs, his plan had been to leave her happy and exhausted, positively aglow from sex. Instead, he'd departed while she was bundled up in a sheet like a hastily wrapped gift, granting him a dispassionate kiss goodbye and leaving him with the crushing sense that they would always have unfinished business.

Another sigh came. He was going to have to stop letting this get to him.

With a long day of client meetings ahead, he decided to get in a workout. He sometimes managed to sneak away at lunch and go to the Sharp and Sharp gym, but that likely wouldn't happen today. He flipped on the light in his master bedroom, grabbed a pair of shorts, a T-shirt and running shoes, then made his way up one set of stairs to the fourth floor of this renovated brownstone. He had a small theater and gym up there, additions he made after his ex-wife moved out. Kelsey never saw the point in watching movies and didn't want the "smell" of a workout space. But now that he was all on his own, Jeremy could do as he liked.

It wasn't much of a consolation.

Forty-five minutes on the treadmill and a half hour of free weights was enough to work up a sufficient sweat and shake off some of the lingering thoughts of Isabel. He hustled down to the second floor and the gourmet kitchen, where he prepared entirely too many meals for one. Coffee was dripping into the carafe when he heard a familiar sound coming from the patio off the back of the house.

Meow.

It was December 9. It was entirely too cold for

an animal to be outside. Jeremy padded over to the glass door, and as had happened many times before, a large orange tabby cat was winding his way back and forth in front of the window. The cat had been to the house many times, and Jeremy had even taken him in once before, over a year ago when it was unbearably hot. The cat's visit had lasted less than a day. He slipped out the front door when Jeremy came home from work that night. Jeremy wasn't a cat person at all—he didn't really see the point of a pet that didn't do anything other than lounge around all day. He'd called Animal Control to see if they could catch him, but they'd seemed unconcerned. He'd even had his assistant call the veterinarian in his neighborhood of Park Slope, but they couldn't do much until someone caught the cat and brought him in. Jeremy kept hoping someone else would take on the burden, but apparently not. At least not today.

Meow. The cat reared up on its hind legs and pressed a single paw to the glass, peering up at Jeremy with eyes that were entirely too plaintive.

Jeremy crouched down and looked into his little cat face. "Buddy. What are you doing out there? It's six in the morning and it's freezing."

Meow. The cat pawed at the glass.

Jeremy straightened. This was the last thing he had time for, but temperatures weren't expected to get above freezing today. He couldn't let the poor thing suffer. Resigned, he flipped the dead bolt, turned the knob and tugged on it. Bitter cold rushed in, but not as fast as the cat. Jeremy closed the door, realizing he now had a big task ahead of him—he had to feed the cat and figure out where to put him all day while he was at work.

He went to the pantry to look for a can of tuna, but that was a bust. Then he remembered that he had some lox in the refrigerator from the bagel shop down the street.

"I guess we're going to find out if you like smoked salmon." He placed a slice of the fish on a plate and broke it into smaller pieces with his fingers. Jeremy had a feeling this was going to be a big hit. The cat was now rubbing against his ankles.

Jeremy put the plate on the floor and the cat began to scarf down the food. Mission one, accomplished. He filled a cereal bowl with water for the cat, then went about making his own breakfast of eggs and a bagel. As he sat at the kitchen island, the cat wound its way around the legs of his barstool, purring loudly enough for Jeremy to hear. He had to get to the office, so he sent a text to his housekeeper, who would be arriving around eight. There's a cat in the house. Don't ask. Can you bring a litter box and show it to him?

Margaret replied quickly. You got a cat?

Jeremy laughed. Not on purpose.

After getting cleaned up and dressed, Jeremy left for the office, arriving promptly at seven thirty, just like every other day. Not only was the weather unbearably cold, it was gray and dreary, somewhat typical for early December, although Jeremy couldn't help but feel like it was somehow sunnier outside than it was inside the Sharp and Sharp offices.

The other partners typically arrived at eight, but Jeremy had learned long ago that his boss, who was also his dad, demanded that his own son deliver more than everyone else. Jeremy had worked twice as hard to make partner. He brought in nearly twice as much billing. He worked like a dog for two reasons. First, he hoped that he would eventually make his father happy enough to loosen his iron grip on the firm and afford Jeremy some autonomy. The second reason fed into the first. When Jeremy had been in the middle of his divorce, he bungled a big case. The Patterson case, a multimillion-dollar wrongful termination suit. It should have been a slam dunk and instead, Jeremy dropped the ball, mostly because his personal life was falling apart. His dad might never forgive him for that grave error, but Jeremy had to keep trying. He had to live the life of a workaholic for the foreseeable future.

In recent months, his father had been pressuring him to bring on a very specific sort of big-fish client, someone with a case that could attract media attention, even of the tabloid variety. In the internet age, one juicy headline brought a lot of free exposure. And although his dad was a traditional and upstanding guy, he loved the spotlight. He basked in it. He loved knowing the firm's coffers were piled to the ceiling with cash.

"Morning, son," his dad said, poking his head into Jeremy's office. He truly was the spitting image of Jeremy, only twenty-three years older. A bit more gray. A few more deep creases. The uncanny similarities in their appearance made the problems in their relationship that much more difficult—on the outside they were nearly identical. On the inside, they couldn't have been more different. "Are we a go with the Summers case?"

"We are. I'm just waiting for the signed agreement to come in this morning and then we'll be in contact with the legal department at Eden's."

His dad glanced at the chair opposite Jeremy's desk. "May I?"

"Of course." Jeremy took a deep breath and prepared himself for what might come—there was no telling with his dad. Some days, he was calm and reasonable. Other times, he hit the roof over the smallest detail. It had been like that since Jeremy was a kid, and he still wasn't used to it.

"What do you think is the real reason Mr. Summers fired Mulvaney and Moore?"

"Honestly? I met with Mr. Summers last night and he's a little off his rocker. He's dead set on getting revenge against the Eden family. This is about far more than money. I'm sure that scared off the senior partners at M and M. They're an incredibly conservative firm." Jeremy leaned back in his chair. "Why? Are you worried about it? There's still time to call it off if you want."

His dad shook his head, pulling at his chin with his fingers. "No. No. I think it's a good thing. Summers is desperate and he's willing to pay for it. I don't have a problem with getting our hands dirty. Your grandfather always avoided it."

Jeremy's grandfather had been the first Sharp in Sharp and Sharp. In fact, Jeremy's dad had declined to add an extra Sharp to the firm's name when Jeremy made partner. He'd simply waited for his own father to pass away. Jeremy missed his grandfather. He was the real reason he'd become an attorney, and things had been much different around the office when he was still alive. His grandfather had a love for the law and the myriad ways it could be interpreted. He loved the arguments and the strategy. His dad had a love of money and winning. He refused to lose, something that had been hammered into Jeremy's head countless times.

"I think it'll be just fine. I have it all under control." Jeremy knew nothing of the sort, but he had to lie. The truth was that the meeting with Benjamin Summers at the Bacharach had been chaotic. Thus the reason for the Manhattan. Thus the reason for perhaps not exercising the best judgment with Isabel.

"Don't let this one get away from you. If he's fired one firm, he'll fire another, and I don't think I need to tell you that it would be a real shame for our bottom line if we lost this billing. It'll be a scramble for you if you have to make up for it."

It was just like his dad to make not-so-thinly-veiled threats. "He's not going to fire us."

"At least you're only going up against the Eden's corporate lawyers. Those guys are so far out of their depth with a case like this. It should be a walk in the park if you do it right."

There went another insult wrapped up as praise. Jeremy wasn't about to point it out. It never did any good. "I'm not worried about it. I've got it all under control."

"Good." His dad rose from his seat and knocked his knuckle against Jeremy's desk, then made his departure. "Have a good day."

"You, too." Jeremy grumbled under his breath and got back to work, writing up the details for his assistant so she could set up the meeting with the Eden's legal team, which he hoped could happen tomorrow. It was the only thing he could do—try to move ahead. Try to make Dad happy. And after that, he'd need to dig into the mountain of work on his desk. Anything to take his mind off Isabel Blackwell and their amazing night that went horribly wrong.

Isabel arrived at Eden's Department Store shortly before 10:00 a.m. the morning after her rendezvous with Jeremy. Her lawyerly instincts normally had her keyed up and wide-awake before a client meeting, but she was so tired she could hardly drag herself out of the taxi.

She hadn't managed more than a few minutes

of sleep. After his departure, Jeremy's warm smell lingered on the sheets, meaning the memory of his touch followed her with every toss and turn. If the condom hadn't broken, their night might have gone on to be nothing less than perfect. He might have asked to see her again, an invitation she would have eagerly accepted. She might have started her new life in New York on a positive note. But the moment they had their mishap and Isabel witnessed firsthand how anxious he was to get out of her room and away from her, she knew he wasn't the right guy. It didn't matter that he was charming, sexy and one of the most handsome men she'd ever had the good fortune to meet. She needed more. She needed a man who would stick around, not run for the exits the instant things got serious.

Per her brother Sam's directions, Isabel took the elevator up to the top floor where the Eden's executive offices were. Sam was sitting in reception when she got there.

"Hey, handsome," she said as Sam got up out of his seat.

He was dressed in all black—suit, shirt and tie, just as most days. He placed a kiss on her forehead. "I'm so glad you're here."

Isabel wasn't quite so happy about it, but she was hopelessly devoted to her brother and that meant she was going to take one last dubious legal assignment before turning her sights to less messy work. "I'm still not sure I'm the right person for this job."

"Are you kidding me? You're the exact right person for this job. You're an expert at making problems like this go away."

The subtext of Sam's words made Isabel's stomach sour. This wasn't the sort of case that got wrapped up by legal wrangling and negotiation. Whenever you had very wealthy, powerful people fighting over something valuable, it inevitably turned into a race to the bottom. Who could dig up the most dirt? Who could make the other side cry for mercy first? "Sam, you know I don't want to tackle this like a fix. I just don't want to work like that anymore."

Sam put his arm around Isabel and snugged her close. "You worry too much. It's just a wealthy guy trying to get his hands on the store. You can handle this in your sleep."

First, I'd have to get some sleep. "But your girlfriend's family legacy is on the line. We can't afford to be cavalier about it."

"You mean fiancée." Mindy Eden appeared on the far side of the reception area and approached them, a big smile on her face.

Isabel knew full well that Sam and Mindy had gotten engaged. She'd merely slipped. Perhaps it was her subconscious reminding her how bothered she was that her younger brother had found the sort of happiness she desperately wanted for herself. "I'm sorry. Fiancée."

Mindy gave Isabel a hug, then wagged her fingers, showing off the square-cut diamond-and-platinum engagement ring Sam had given her. The thing was so big it looked like Mindy was walking around with an ice cube on her hand. "I honestly never thought this would happen."

Isabel didn't believe that for a minute. Mindy was lovely, but she seemed like the sort of woman who was accustomed to nothing less than getting exactly what she wanted out of life. "Why's that? You had to know my brother was over the moon for you."

Mindy elbowed Sam in the ribs. "I was oblivious to that for a while. I spent so much time focused on my career that I forgot to open my eyes."

Isabel took a shred of comfort in that. She and Mindy might have butted heads when they first met, but that was only because of Isabel's protectiveness of Sam. Mindy had hurt him and Isabel wasn't going to be the one to forgive her for it. Now that Sam and Mindy had reconciled, and the two women had gotten to know each other a little better, Isabel knew that she and Mindy had some things in common. They were both driven, determined and not willing to take crap from anyone. "I'll try to remember that when I jump back into the dating pool."

"Any prospects?" Mindy asked.

"I'm out of here if you're going to talk about guys," Sam said, turning away. "I don't do well with this subject when it comes to my sister."

Isabel grabbed his arm. "Oh, stop. We're not going to talk about that because there's nothing to say. I need to get an apartment. There are a million other things for me to accomplish before I can seriously think about dating. I have to find an office and get my new practice up and running."

"Don't put it off too long," Mindy said. She then cast her sights at Sam. "Are there any cute, eligible guys working for you right now? Maybe you can set her up."

Sam shook his head. "Something tells me she doesn't want that."

In truth, Isabel might not mind it. If Sam picked out a man for her, she'd not only know that he had been fully vetted, she'd have the knowledge that Sam approved. That was no small matter. "We'll see how I do. For now, let's sit down and talk about the case." Isabel was resigned to moving forward with this, and the sooner she started, the sooner she'd be done. So she'd delay her fresh start a few weeks. It wasn't the end of the world.

"Come on," Mindy said. "We're going to meet in Emma's office. It's the biggest. It used to belong to my gram."

Gram, or Victoria Eden, was the founder of Eden's Department Store, which at its height had more than fifty stores worldwide. Unfortunately, the chain was now down to a single location, the original Manhattan store. Mrs. Eden had passed away unexpectedly a little more than a year ago, and left the business to Mindy, her sister, Sophie, and their half sister, Emma. It was a bit of a tawdry story— all three women had the same father, and their two mothers were also sisters. Victoria Eden had brought the affair to light via her will, where she told everyone of her son's dalliance in an attempt to give Emma some justice.

Inside the office, Emma and Sophie were waiting. Isabel had met them both at a fund-raiser a month and a half ago, which was also when Sam and Mindy had finally figured out that they were desperately in love. Mindy made reintroductions and they all sat in the seating area—Isabel and Sophie on the couch, Sam in one chair with Mindy perched on the arm, and Emma opposite them.

"I guess we need to walk you through as much of this as we know," Mindy said. "I wish we had more information, but until a few weeks ago, we had no idea who Benjamin Summers was."

"He claims that our grandmother had an affair with his father, which is utterly preposterous," Sophie said. "Gram was devoted to our grandfather for as long as he was alive."

"Please, Soph. Can you not do this right now? Let me finish," Mindy said, returning her sights to Isabel. "This would have been nearly forty years ago if it really happened. Early days for the store, but our grandmother was doing well and by all accounts, very eager to expand. That's when Mr. Summers, the father, comes into play. Supposedly he lent our grandmother a quarter of a million dollars so she could open additional locations."

"That was a lot of money at that time," Isabel said. "And this is a handwritten promissory note?"

"Yes," Mindy said. "We've been going back through the store's old financials and bank records, but we can't find any record of an influx of money. There are large chunks of cash flowing into the store at that time, but it could have just been sales. Unfortunately, the accounting from that time is nowhere near as exact as it is now. Most of it is on paper."

Isabel's gears were starting to turn. As much as she'd said she didn't want to do this sort of work anymore—untangling the pasts of wealthy people— she had to admit that she had a real knack for it, and that made her feel as though she was ready to tackle it. "The first thing we're going to need to do is get the promissory note authenticated. There's a good chance it's not real."

"Do you think it could be a fake?" Emma asked.

"You'd be surprised the lengths people will go to in order to cash in."

"But Mr. Summers is so wealthy," Mindy said. "Why would he do that?"

Isabel sat back and crossed her legs. "It might not be the cash. It might be the store he's after."

"No. We can't let that happen," Sophie blurted.

Isabel didn't want to be the bearer of bad tidings. Losing the store was a real possibility. For now, Isabel needed to get up to speed on the materials in the case and see where the Eden sisters stood. "Let's not get ahead of ourselves. Give me some time to look over everything. I have several different financial detectives I've worked with in the past. They're going to need access to your records to see if we can figure out if the money ever flowed into the store at all."

"How long is all of that going to take?" Mindy asked.

"A few days to a few weeks. It just depends."

Mindy cleared her throat and Isabel sensed something bad was about to come to light. "Yeah. About that. We don't have that kind of time. Mr. Summers's lawyer sent a letter to the Eden's in-house counsel today. He's threatening a lawsuit right away if we don't come to the negotiating table tomorrow."

Isabel blinked several times while trying to absorb what Mindy had just said. "Mr. Summers not only wants us to start negotiating tomorrow, his lawyer isn't even aware the store is employing outside counsel?"

"We thought a sneak attack was the best approach. They're expecting someone else. Not Isabel Blackwell, Washington, DC, fixer."

Isabel cringed at the words. She didn't want to be that person anymore.

Sam sat forward and placed his hand on his sister's knee. "I have to agree. The store is too important to the Eden family for us to be anything less than completely strategic about this. They'll prepare for a corporate negotiation, not having any idea who they're dealing with."

Isabel took a deep breath, trying to ignore the way

her already soured stomach grew even more uneasy. "Can I see the letter they sent?"

"Yes. Of course." Mindy hopped up from her seat and grabbed a thin folder from Emma's desk, handing it to Isabel.

Inside was a single page—the letter inviting Eden's Department Store's legal representation to the negotiating table. All looked in order until Isabel saw the name on the signature line. Then the blood drained from her face.

Jeremy Sharp. Oh my God.

Her big meeting tomorrow with the lawyer representing the man who wanted to take down Eden's Department Store? It would be the second run-in with her one-night stand. And apparently, they were about to go from the bedroom to the war room.

Four

"I don't want you to worry," Jeremy said as he escorted Benjamin Summers into one of the meeting rooms at Sharp and Sharp. "We have everything well in hand."

Mr. Summers turned to Jeremy and narrowed his eyes until they were only small slits. "Why aren't we meeting in the main conference room? The one with the big windows. The one you can see from the waiting room."

Jeremy pulled back a chair and offered Mr. Summers a seat. "Because this is more discreet." In truth, Jeremy preferred it because it meant his father couldn't interfere unless he walked right in on them. Jeremy had been in many client meetings where his dad paced back and forth outside that main conference room. It was unnerving as hell.

Mr. Summers sat in a huff. Jeremy hadn't spent a lot of time with him, but he'd always been like this— gruff and impatient. "I'm not worried about discretion. If anything, I'd prefer not to have it. I'd like the whole world to know that I'm going after Eden's. Victoria Eden destroyed my parents' marriage and this is the only way I can seek retribution on behalf of my mother."

Jeremy poured Mr. Summers a glass of water, hoping that might help to cool his temper. "I don't think it's a great idea to bring that up in this meeting. I know it's difficult to curb your personal feelings about the matter, but we need to focus on the bottom line, which is a very large unpaid debt."

Mr. Summers cleared his throat and tapped his fingers on the table. "Fine. I'll take your advice."

"Thank you. I appreciate that."

"For now."

One of the admins in the office poked his head into the conference room. "Mr. Sharp, the Eden's representatives and legal team have arrived. Shall I show them in?"

Jeremy turned to Mr. Summers, hoping he could get him to remain calm and collected. "Are you ready, Mr. Summers?"

"More than I've ever been."

Jeremy stood and straightened his jacket, then made his way to the door. The in-house counsel for

Eden's was a crew of white-haired older men, much like his dad and Mr. Summers. He knew he could handle this easily as long as everyone could set aside their egos. But when he glanced down the hall, a stunning vision came into view—a woman who was not easy to handle. *Isabel.*

What the hell? For an instant, Jeremy shrank back from the door, his mind whirring with thoughts, even when there was no time to think. Before he knew what was happening, Isabel, along with another woman and a very tall man, were being led into the room by Jeremy's admin. "Mr. Sharp, this is Mindy Eden, COO of Eden's Department Store."

Mindy, willowy and poised with flame-red hair, offered her hand. "Mr. Sharp."

"Special adviser to Eden's, Sam Blackwell," his admin continued.

Sam, towering and dressed in black, shook Jeremy's hand. "Hello."

"And lastly, Isabel Blackwell, special counsel for Eden's."

Isabel stepped forward, but her beguiling scent arrived a split second before her. It filled his nose, and that sent memories storming into his mind— their white-hot tryst in her hotel room was not anything he would forget anytime soon. Unfortunately, he couldn't afford to think about what her luscious naked body looked like under her trim gray suit. He was too busy trying to tamp down his inner confusion. Had she known who he was when she seduced him? Had she seen him in the bar with Mr. Summers a mere fifteen minutes before the fire alarm sounded?

"It's nice to meet you." Isabel offered her hand. He'd noticed that night that her skin was unusually warm, but right now he felt as though he'd been burned.

Jeremy cleared his throat. "Nice to meet *you*, as well." He gestured to the other side of the long mahogany table, more rattled than when he'd worked his very first case. He couldn't help but feel as though they were being ambushed. He'd been led to believe that Eden's in-house counsel would be handling this. Unless Isabel was a new addition to their team, she was a ringer. "Please have a seat."

Isabel sat directly opposite Jeremy. The look on her face was difficult to decipher, but he reminded himself that he hardly knew her. What were her motives? What sort of person was she? Most important, what was her endgame? For a man with countless trust issues when it came to women, this was not only bringing all that to the surface in an uncomfortable way, it felt as though Isabel had opened an entirely new area of mistrust to explore. He deeply disliked the revelation.

Jeremy drew in a calming breath. *Focus.* He looked Isabel square in the eye. She met his gaze with steely composure. On the surface, she was quite simply stunning. Easily the sexiest woman he'd ever met. But he sensed now that beneath that flawless exterior was a woman who was at the very least, trouble. He didn't want to regret the other night, but perhaps he should. Would he feel as though he was at less of a disadvantage right now if it hadn't happened? "Ms. Blackwell, your client's grandmother borrowed 250 million dollars from Mr. Summers's father in 1982. She offered the Manhattan location of Eden's Department Store, the building, inventory and the land it sits on as collateral. By our calculations, with standard interest adjusted for inflation and compounded monthly, that unpaid loan now sits at a balance of just over 842 million."

"You have got to be kidding," Mindy Eden scoffed. "Why not just round it up to an even billion?"

Isabel placed her hand on Mindy's forearm, then smiled at Jeremy, the picture of cool composure. "And what exactly would Mr. Summers like for us to do about that?"

Jeremy had no choice but to continue. "As it's been nearly forty years, Mr. Summers expects the loan to be repaid in cash within thirty days or we'll begin proceedings to claim the property."

Isabel nodded, then licked her lips, making Jeremy clutch the arm of his chair. "Any talk of property seizure is premature, Mr. Sharp. Frankly, my client had never even heard of Mr. Summers prior to the letter your team sent to the Eden's offices, so I don't know how the Eden family should be expected to simply hand over the keys to a multibillion-dollar business and property without exploring this matter as thoroughly as possible."

Jeremy knew he should be feeling as though he'd been put on notice, but he only felt incredibly turned on. Blood was coursing through his body so fast it was making his head swim. Oh, Isabel was good.

"My first priority is to determine the authenticity of the promissory note," Isabel continued, her cheeks flushed with brilliant pink. "We can't be expected to proceed without an expert analysis of the document. I'm not convinced it's authentic or that it has Victoria Eden's true signature on it."

This was not good news. And yet Jeremy noticed a significant tightening in his pants.

"Are you calling me a liar?" Mr. Summers bellowed.

Jeremy turned to his client. "Please, Ben," he muttered. "I've got this."

"It's a handwritten note, Mr. Summers." Isabel's voice was direct and cutting, while her chest was heaving in a way that brought back entirely too many memories of the night at the Bacharach—having Isabel at his mercy, in her bed. "Anyone could have produced it. You could have fabricated it last week for all we know."

"It's real. I have no reason to lie," Benjamin said.

Isabel's eyebrows shot up. "From where I'm sitting, you have 842 million reasons to lie. Do you have financial problems I should know about, Mr.

Summers? Is that what I'm going to find when I start looking into your businesses?"

"Ms. Blackwell," Jeremy said as a warning, stopping himself from uttering what he really wanted to say—*Ms. Blackwell, you and I need to hash this out on our own. Alone. On this conference table.* But he had to get his act together. "Ms. Blackwell, I'll thank you not to speak to my client directly, especially when you're accusing him of things that have no basis in fact. Mr. Summers is not on trial here."

"If he's going to get ugly about the matter in front of my client, I'm afraid I have no other choice. This is not as cut-and-dried as you're trying to paint it."

Jeremy sensed this meeting was starting to go off the rails and he had to get it back on track. More than anything, he really needed to ask Isabel a few questions that were not appropriate in front of their respective clients. "Ms. Blackwell, would you mind asking your clients to wait out in the lobby? I'll ask Mr. Summers to adjourn to my office so that you and I can discuss the terms of determining the authenticity of the note."

Isabel lifted her chin and narrowed her sights on Jeremy, seeming suspicious. "I'll give you five minutes."

I'd rather have ten. "Certainly."

Isabel turned to Mindy and Sam, and they conferred with heads bowed. Jeremy took his chance to chat with Mr. Summers.

"I don't like being taken out of the negotiations," Mr. Summers said in response.

"I assure you, this will be nothing more than boring legalese. Plus, it'll give me a chance to find out more of what exactly their strategy is. This isn't the usual Eden's team."

"It isn't? I expect my lawyer to know details like that."

Jeremy looked over at Isabel as she got up from the table and made way for Mindy and Sam to leave the conference room. "In my experience, these things rarely go the way you think they will."

Isabel accompanied Sam and Mindy out to the luxe Sharp and Sharp lobby. With dark wood, soft light and tufted navy leather settees, it spoke of old money and an organization steeped in tradition. Isabel could only imagine how her life would have been different if she'd come to New York instead of Washington, DC, and gotten her start at a firm like this, where business was done aboveboard. Sure, Mr. Summers had made a spectacle in the meeting, but it was nothing more than a man, accustomed to getting everything he wanted, kicking up dust because she and the Eden family were not going to go down without a fight. It wasn't a real roll in the mud, one where people make threats to destroy other people's lives.

"Is this normal?" Sam whispered at Isabel. His body language suggested pure agitation. His back was stiff as a board. "For the other lawyer to kick everybody out of the room?"

Isabel surveyed the lobby, which was unoccupied

except for the receptionist, who was on the phone. If they were going to discuss this, they needed privacy. She placed her hand on Sam's arm. She wasn't entirely sure what Jeremy's motives were, but she was curious. Their short string of quipping back and forth had really gotten her running hot. And damn, the man could rock a suit unlike any other. "I think he was trying to get his client to cool down. Which I think is for the best. Plus, I didn't want him saying anything disparaging in front of Mindy."

"Why?" Mindy asked. "You know I can take it."

Isabel laughed quietly. "I know you can. It's more that we need to walk a fine line between being tough and not escalating anything. Summers and Sharp are going to be all about taking things up a notch. It's my job to walk everything back."

"But you were the one who threatened to look into his business," Mindy said.

"I know. He still needs to know we're serious. And I had to let him know that I won't hestiate to call his bluff." What Isabel really meant to say was that old habits died hard.

Sam turned to Mindy. "I thought that was a brilliant move, personally. We need to fight fire with fire. We need to dig up dirt on this Summers guy and it's not a bad idea to go after his lawyer, too. I don't like that guy. He's smug and arrogant, the exact kind of guy I'd love to take down a notch."

Mindy looked at Sam like he had a screw loose.

"Do you seriously not know who that guy is? Jeremy Sharp? Ex-husband of Kelsey Kline? The socialite?"

"Shh, you two," Isabel snapped, eying the receptionist, who thankfully hadn't seemed to overhear their conversation. Still, Isabel's mind was reeling. Jeremy had been married? And to a socialite? Both details came as a big surprise, but Isabel had fought her urge to look into his personal life when she learned that he was handling the case for Mr. Summers. Only the old Isabel did that. Now she might have no choice but to do at least a minimum of digging. Otherwise, she'd die of curiosity. She glanced at her brother. How could she tell Sam that the man he found so unlikable was someone she'd fallen into bed with? Sam would never judge her for it, but he would be disappointed, and as far as Isabel was concerned, that was worse.

"Sorry." Sam shoved his hands into his pockets. "I'm stressed. I hate that Mindy has to go through this."

"It's okay," Isabel offered, loving that her brother was so focused on Mindy's well-being. "Look, let's focus on the merits of the case. We need to get an expert to analyze the promissory note and make sure it's legitimate. I've already hired the financial forensic experts. They're going through the old Eden's books to see if there's any evidence the money flowed through the store." She turned to Mindy. "And I was thinking, if this relationship between Mr. Summers's dad and your grandmother was this significant, don't you think there'd likely be some evidence of it somewhere in her personal effects? Maybe old papers? Letters of some sort?"

"I got Gram's apartment after she passed away, but I never moved in. I had planned to, but it's only been a year and, well…" Mindy looked at Sam with utter adoration. "Your brother came along and everything changed."

"Our offer was accepted on the house out in New Jersey," Sam said to Isabel.

"It's way too much room for two people," Mindy added with a smile that said it didn't bother her at all.

Sam shrugged it off, but his grin was also a mile wide. "I want us to start having kids as soon as possible. I've put my life on hold for too long. And I've always wanted a family."

Isabel understood exactly what Sam was saying. She wanted those things for herself. In many ways, she felt like she and Sam would never truly heal from the trauma of losing their parents until they were each able to start a family.

"I'd still like to get married first," Mindy offered.

If these two were going to continue to ruminate about their shared future, Isabel would never get any work done today. "Mindy, if you and I could get together and go through your grandmother's apartment, that would be great. In the meantime, I need to go back in there and hash things out with Mr. Sharp."

"Unless you need us, I think we'll take off and grab lunch," Sam said.

Isabel nodded. "Excellent idea."

Mindy hooked her arm in Sam's. "Thank you, Isabel, for having our backs. My sisters and I appreciate it more than you will ever know. Something about having a woman in charge makes us all breathe a little easier."

Sam's forehead crinkled in confusion. "I realize she's an amazing lawyer, but what does being a woman have to do with it?"

It was apparent Mindy was doing her best not to roll her eyes. "I like to be in control, and your sister and I are a lot alike. I know that she won't allow herself to fail. She'll keep at it until we win. She won't try to settle."

Winning was Isabel's preferred result, but this case wasn't going to be that simple. And her brief history with Jeremy would certainly complicate it. "There will have to be some negotiation, Mindy. That's just the way it works," Isabel said. She didn't make a habit of lowering her own bar, but if the note was determined to be authentic, Eden's was in a very difficult situation, one that Isabel would have to work miracles to get them out of.

"*If* the note is real," Mindy said. "I think there's a good chance that this is all a hoax."

Isabel could only hope for that right now. "I'd better get back in there and get it settled." She straightened her jacket and strode back down the hall. Wanting to appear confident and strong, she marched right into the room. And right into Jeremy. She reflexively braced herself, planting her hands on his chest. He gripped her elbows. She gazed up into his soft gray eyes. He intently peered down into hers. Her lips twitched with electricity, their connection fiercely uncomfortable to endure. Of course she'd fallen into bed with him that first night. Of course they'd given in to this. It would be impossible not to.

But now they were standing in a law office with a messy case to unravel. This was no time for rubbing up against Jeremy.

However badly she wanted to do exactly that.

She dropped her hands, and he dropped his, creating distance by stepping away. Isabel stared at the carpet, a perfectly ordinary office gray, as she struggled to regain her composure. She wasn't regretting the fact that they'd slept together. She found herself again regretting that she'd ever taken on this case.

"Sorry," Isabel said. "I guess I was in a hurry for us to get back to work."

Jeremy cleared his throat. "As am I. Lord only knows what Mr. Summers might do if left to his own devices in my office for too long." He flashed a quick smile at her. "Kidding, of course. He's fine in there." He strode to the door and closed it.

Isabel swallowed hard. Something about the sight of his hand against the ebony wood made her pulse skip a beat. She needed to get a grip. She was in the throes of battle with this man. Constantly reminding herself how sexy he was would only put her at a disadvantage. It didn't matter that he smelled good enough to eat. It didn't matter how unbelievable he looked in that suit.

"So," he started. "I take it this is why you didn't want to discuss your career the other night? Very clever of you."

"That wasn't the reason. I truly didn't want to talk about work. Is that so odd?"

"For someone who seems so eager to embrace her role as attorney, I find that a little peculiar."

"Eager? I'm just doing my job." She sat down and crossed her legs, hyperaware of the way her skirt hitched up an inch too far. She tugged at the hem as inconspicuously as possible. She needed to wrestle her side of their sexual tension into submission. It wasn't good for her or her client.

"Well, I have to admit that you're good at it. Very good." Jeremy sat down and drew a circle on the table with his index finger, making eye contact with her the whole time. Her mind zipped back to the memory of his hands on her naked skin—her breasts, her butt, her most delicate places—the parts that made her want him just as bad now as she had the other night. If only things hadn't ended so disastrously. "I got a little worked up there. You're definitely the most interesting person I've had the chance to spar with in recent history."

Isabel had always been drawn to that side of the law, where you make an argument, the other side responds with their own, and it then becomes a battle of wills, each party strengthening their stance until someone has no choice but to beg for mercy. Of course, it only felt good to come out on top. It felt horrible to lose. "Hopefully there won't have to be too much of that. I'd like to come to an agreement, starting with getting that note authenticated."

Just then the door flew open and a handsome, well-dressed older man stormed in. The resemblance to Jeremy was striking. It was like someone had hit the fast-forward button twenty years.

"Excuse me." The man barely glanced at Isabel. "Jeremy, can I speak with you?"

Jeremy impatiently rose from his seat, so fast that the chair rolled and hit the table with a thud. "We're in the middle of something. Can't this wait?"

"Why is Mr. Summers in your office?"

"He can't keep himself in line, that's why," Jeremy whispered, but it was loud enough for Isabel to hear every word.

The man unsubtly eyed Isabel, then returned his sights to Jeremy. "I'll go have a chat with him."

"Please don't."

Jeremy's voice was exceptionally firm, sending a thrill through Isabel, one she tried to ignore. She pulled out a legal pad and made a few scribbles to distract herself.

"All right then," the man said. "Check in with me when you're finished."

Jeremy said nothing in response as the man exited the room, but he had that stressed look on his face—the same one he'd had when he left Isabel's hotel room. "I'm sorry about that. My dad. He's supposed to be in partial retirement, but it only means that he has fewer clients but spends just as much time in the office."

"Leaving him too much time to interfere with what you're doing?" Isabel asked.

"Yes. Precisely."

Isabel didn't know much about Jeremy other than the revelation from Mindy that he'd been married, and apparently to a woman of some social stature, but she did feel bad that his own father was causing him distress. "No worries. Let's get back to the authentication. I've only been in New York a few weeks, so I don't have an expert on hand in the city. I know several in DC. I'm happy to bring one up."

"DC, huh? Big Washington lawyer?"

"Not exactly." Isabel pressed her lips together tightly.

"Something tells me you're underselling yourself." Jeremy's phone beeped with a text. "I'm so sorry, but I've been waiting for a message. Do you mind?"

"No. Of course not."

Jeremy pulled his phone from his pocket, seeming concerned. "Do you think we could discuss the authentication of the letter over dinner? I actually have to run home right now."

Run home during the day? Did Jeremy have a family? A girlfriend? He was becoming more of a puzzle by the moment. "I hope everything's okay."

He sighed heavily. "I think so. I ended up taking in a stray cat. It's a long story."

"Sounds like a lot."

"It's like everything in my life right now. Just one more thing on an endless list of obligations."

Isabel nodded, a bit chagrined that she'd been so right about Jeremy—he was not the guy who liked to be tied down. "Okay, then. You can tell me over dinner. Eight o'clock? The Monaco?"

Jeremy looked surprised. "It's impossible to get a reservation."

Isabel shrugged. "I know a guy."

"But you've only been in the city for a few weeks."

"Trust me. I got this."

Five

Dinner with Jeremy—hot and absurdly handsome Jeremy—was not the best plan. To some, it might seem like a particularly poor one. Did Isabel have a choice? Of course she did. She never liked to think that she didn't. But wrapping up this case on Mr. Summers's proposed timeline would take some artful work on Isabel's part if she was going to come out on top. For herself, her brother and his new family, she wanted nothing less than a win.

She did not want to be quibbling with this in January or having it drag out into February or March. She wanted this done so she could move on to the next phase of her career, adoption law. It would be a lot easier to get something out of Jeremy if the two of them had a good rapport, and well, the way things had played out at the Bacharach the night they met had not been a great start. She wanted to put that behind them, and in her experience, nothing cured a few bruised feelings faster than a glass of wine and some conversation over a delicious meal. Plus, the pasta carbonara at the Monaco was to die for.

First, she needed to get back to the Bacharach from the Sharp and Sharp offices. Wanting to clear her head, she opted to walk, even if she had to do it in heels. A crisp December wind whipped between the tall buildings of Midtown Manhattan, bringing Isabel the focus she craved. All around her, the city was abuzz with the holidays. She strode past storefronts with extravagant window displays, hosting scenes of Santa and snowy ski chalets, candy canes and snowflakes. Red-cheeked shoppers bustled along the sidewalk, loaded down with department store bags, including silver-and-white bags from Eden's, which was only seven or eight blocks away. Isabel hadn't celebrated Christmas in years. Well, not for real, with a tree and gifts and the Wham! song some people try to avoid hearing. She and Sam typically got together on Christmas Eve and spent a few quiet days together, cooking and talking, content with each other's company. It had been like that since their parents died, when Sam was in high school and Isabel in college. The holiday simply didn't have the same meaning without their entire family together. Losing both parents in a six-month period had left them no time to adjust. So she and Sam slipped into a new tradition, made up of celebrating the one thing they still had—each other.

Isabel wasn't sure what would happen this year. Sam had Mindy now. With that big lovely ring on her finger, they were buying their big house and talking about children. Of course, Isabel was over the moon about the whole thing. Yes, she'd been reluctant to accept Mindy after the heartbreak she'd caused Sam, but in the end, she'd been won over by Mindy's magnetic personality and determination. Plus, Isabel had to be nothing but in awe of her future sister-in-law. She'd accomplished the impossible, something no one else had managed in his thirty-six years on this planet— Mindy had found a way to make Sam happy.

Isabel arrived back at the Bacharach and dashed in through the revolving door, crossed the lobby and pressed the button for the elevator. She couldn't help but notice the woman in the fire department uniform speaking to the man she knew to be the hotel manager.

"The entire system?" the manager asked.

"I'm afraid so, sir. One minute it passes the test, the next minute it fails."

The elevator dinged and Isabel didn't hang around to hear more about the hotel's faulty alarm system. Hopefully it would get fixed soon.

Upstairs, she keyed into her room, unwound herself from her black wool coat, which she tossed onto the bed. She kicked off her pumps, sat at the desk and opened her laptop. She probably should have just given in to the urge to look into Jeremy yesterday, when she first learned that her one-night stand was opposing counsel. Less than a second after hitting the return button on *Jeremy Sharp*, a flurry of tabloid articles appeared. The first headline suggested exactly what Mindy had: Kelsey Kline Leaves Husband, Says Marriage "Loveless."

Isabel wasn't much for pulp or gossip, and she'd never even heard of Kelsey Kline before that morning, but the story was fascinating. The only daughter of a shipping magnate, heiress to a vast fortune, Ms. Kline was well-known in NYC as a party girl turned fashion blogger turned wedding planner. She was flat-out gorgeous, fit yet curvy, with high cheekbones, full lips and a stunning head of chocolate-brown hair. Isabel didn't know Jeremy particularly well, but Kelsey seemed like the kind of woman he might choose—fun and carefree.

As Isabel read on, the story turned dark and sad. Kelsey claimed that Jeremy was inattentive and unaffectionate, not the marrying type or a guy who was meant to settle down. She said point-blank that he broke her heart, getting married to him was a mistake, and she might never recover. There were even a few hints that he might have been unfaithful, although it was a subject carefully tiptoed around. No matter whether that was true or not, this was all another sign that Isabel might have dodged a bullet.

Kelsey filed for divorce less than three years after

she and Jeremy had tied the knot in a lavish ceremony at a historic cathedral in the city. Other than
being blamed for the end of the marriage, Jeremy
was hardly mentioned in the article at all. It said that
he had declined to comment, which Isabel took as
confirmation that everything Kelsey had said was
true, at least on some level. Otherwise, why not stick
up for yourself?

Isabel took in a deep breath through her nose and
closed her laptop, not wanting to read any more. She
felt that familiar crawl over her skin after having
peered into someone else's life. She realized there
were plenty of people who lived for such salacious
details, but Isabel had seen too much of the personal
toll. At least she was now certain that she had made
the right call when she'd let Jeremy off the hook
after their first night together. She would have dinner with him tonight, get this case worked out and
move on. That would be the end of her chapter with
Mr. Sharp. And from the sound of that article, that
was the best case scenario.

A few minutes before eight, Isabel climbed out of
a town car in front of the Monaco. From the outside,
the restaurant was a mystery—a dark wood facade
with a large arched center door, the name in gold
above. No random passersby would ever bother to
step inside unprompted, out of either ignorance or
perhaps fear of the unknown. But it was one of Isabel's favorite spots in Manhattan, owned by a for-

mer client who had top-tier restaurants all over the world—London, Madrid, Los Angeles, DC. Isabel's last assignment for the restaurateur had been to get his college-age daughter out of jail when she was arrested in Belize on spring break. It had been Isabel's job to not only deal with the legal side of getting her out and back into the US, but to keep the story out of the papers and away from her university. Thus had been her life of a lawyer turned fixer.

Isabel ducked through the door and into a dimly lit vestibule with an ornate tile floor, coat check and host stand. The sounds of the restaurant, a steady hum of conversation and clinking glass, filtered into the small space, even through the heavy emerald-green velvet drape that obscured the entrance into the dining room. Isabel gave her name to the hostess just as a rush of cold came in behind her. She turned and there was Jeremy. He was clearly flustered, his cheeks full of color as he pushed his hair back from his face. Isabel endeavored to ignore the way her pulse raced when she saw him. He turned his shoulders out of a charcoal-gray wool coat, dressed in black trousers and suit jacket, with a midnight-blue dress shirt that turned his gray eyes an even darker and more intense shade. Isabel had to hope that at some point the zap of attraction would subside. Hopefully it wouldn't always feel like this to be around him, as if her body was on perpetual high alert.

"Everything okay?" she asked.

He smiled thinly. "Basically, yes. Just a crazy afternoon."

"Crazy good or crazy bad?"

He blew out a breath. "The stray cat I told you about? I thought it was a male, but it's a female. And she's pregnant."

Isabel pressed her lips together tightly to stifle a laugh. For the guy who seemed to be bothered by responsibility, this was pretty funny. "What are you going to do?"

"I'm going to buy you a drink as soon as we're seated for dinner. That's what."

Isabel signaled the hostess with a nod and they were led into the restaurant, just as beautiful as she'd remembered it, with its signature emerald-green circular booths for two, soft lighting and glamorous clientele. Jeremy waited for Isabel to sit before he slid into the other side of the booth. It was a sexy and intimate setting, perfect if there had been the possibility of any romance between them at all. But the article she'd read a few hours ago had put that idea to rest. Instead, she hoped to lean on the privacy of their table to start cutting their deal. They each ordered a drink from their server—a gin and tonic for Isabel and a Manhattan for Jeremy.

"I haven't been here in years," Jeremy said, flipping through the menu. Isabel already knew what she was going to order: her favorite pasta. "It's pretty much a date-night spot."

Isabel hadn't considered the possibility that Jeremy

might have memories of this place with his ex-wife. Or other women. Her mind then made the next leap—did he think she was trying to make a romantic overture? She deeply hoped that was not the case. She didn't want to embarrass herself. "I love the food, though. It's exceptional."

"Indeed."

Their drinks were quickly delivered and they placed their dinner orders. "I suppose a toast is in order," Jeremy said once the server had left. "To making a deal."

Isabel was happy to hear that Jeremy didn't have romance on the brain. It might make it easier for her to set aside the thoughts that kept creeping into her consciousness—sharing a drink brought back too many memories of their blazing-hot first kiss. "Yes." She took a sip and placed her glass back on the table. "So, the authentication of the promissory note. Do you have an expert we can call on? I'd like to speak to them, of course, and have a detailed outline of their process, their experience in the field, and have them sign an agreement of impartiality."

"I have one person we work with, but I can assure you that they'll do a great job and they'll get it done quickly."

"We wouldn't want to mess with Mr. Summers and his thirty-day timeline."

"We're already nearly a week in. The clock started the day we sent the first letter. And you can't blame the guy. The loan is long overdue."

"And my clients had no idea the loan ever existed. You can't pay off what you don't know about."

"They don't seem eager to repay it now."

Isabel stirred her drink. "It's not a simple matter to pull that kind of cash together at one time. Especially not with so little time."

Jeremy shrugged it off. "I don't want to sound like a jerk, but it's not my problem."

Isabel did not like the way this was going. She saw too little room for negotiation. This case might be even tougher than she'd thought. "I would never say you sound like a jerk. But you do sound like the lawyer of a jerk."

Despite being referred to as the lawyer of a jerk, being out with Isabel was far more enjoyable than the many work-related obligations Jeremy endured on any given week. "If that's what I am, at least it pays the bills."

"Good to know you have your priorities," she said, then took a long sip of her drink.

Jeremy had to hide his amusement as the waiter delivered their meals. Isabel was a far cry from the usual blowhard attorney. He genuinely enjoyed her company. She was more than simply beautiful and smart. The world seemed different around her, the air charged with mystery and excitement. Jeremy had learned a lot about her after she'd left his office that afternoon. While working in Washington, DC, she'd gathered a passel of high-powered clients—senators, billionaires and cabinet officials. Not a single controversy or scandal seemed to stick to any of them, even when lawsuits were filed and whistles were blown. Accusations and rumors all vanished into thin air, and Jeremy was smart enough to know that didn't happen on its own. Did Isabel's beautiful exterior and graceful facade make it easier for her to sweep things under the rug or keep secrets? If so, it made her even more dangerous than he'd thought that morning. "So, I have to ask, why didn't you call me as soon as you realized that I was the opposing counsel? That part of this whole thing seems especially sneaky."

Isabel dabbed at the corners of her stunning mouth with a napkin. He had an improper desire to kiss her until her lipstick was gone. Despite being on opposite sides of the negotiating table, that sexual energy between them wasn't going anywhere. "Honestly?"

"Please. I don't do well with anything less." Jeremy found himself cutting his steak a little more aggressively than was warranted. Even the manipulation of words bothered him, which made being a lawyer difficult. So much of the job was about the careful parsing of language.

"It was my brother Sam's idea. He thought it would give us an advantage if you didn't know who exactly you would be facing. I apologize if you felt ambushed, but it was just a tactic."

That morning in his office had likely only been

Jeremy's first taste of the sorts of things to which Isabel might resort. "It made me look like an ass in front of my client. I certainly don't appreciate that."

Isabel nodded. "Fair enough. I guess it wasn't the kindest thing to do. Sam is just very protective of his fiancée, Mindy, and the entire Eden family for that matter. And since it's just Sam and me in our family, I guess that I'm part of that scenario, too."

Jeremy understood family loyalty, but only to a point. If his grandfather were still alive, he'd still have undying devotion to the Sharp name. But his parents certainly didn't inspire that sort of allegiance. They'd treated him horribly in the aftermath of his divorce, more preoccupied by the public embarrassment than the fact that their son had experienced a great personal betrayal. "Do you actually like working for the Eden family?"

Isabel shot him a quizzical look. "That's a loaded question."

"Why?"

"The tone of your voice for starters. You sound as though the Eden family disgusts you."

Jeremy was letting his personal bias get in the way, but he couldn't help it. The Eden family and his ex's family seemed to be very much the same— wealthy beyond measure, treating the world as their personal playground. "It's just the entitlement. It drives me crazy. The Eden sisters have been handed a vast fortune and now they're quibbling over this debt. I assure you that Mr. Summers would not dredge up this matter if he didn't desperately want it resolved. It's a very personal thing for him. The affair between Victoria Eden and his father destroyed his family. I don't think we can discount the personal component of the case."

Isabel set her fork down on her plate. "And surely you know it takes two people to tango. Mr. Summers seems to want to assign all blame to Victoria Eden. He wants to paint her as a home-wrecker, when the reality is that his own father was complicit as well if the affair happened as he says it did. For all we know, his father could have instigated the whole thing."

Jeremy felt his pulse pick up. His heart hammered. He did love it when Isabel delivered a smart jab, even if he was on the receiving end of it.

"*If* the affair actually happened," she continued. "We don't know that for sure."

She bit down on her lip, her dark eyes scanning his face. Damn, her skin was beautiful in this soft light and all he could think was how badly he wanted to touch it. To touch her. Every inch. He wasn't the type of guy to rest too much of his self-worth on how things went in the bedroom, but he was certain that he had rocked Isabel's world during their one evening together, and it was still aggravating him that it had ended on such an inelegant note.

She shook her head and looked down at the table, her dark hair falling across her face. "I'm sorry. I just get worked up. I don't like seeing a woman shouldering the blame for this. Men and women are equal and should be treated as such, good or bad."

"Don't apologize for your anger. I'd much rather go up against someone with some passion behind what they do than deal with a robot."

Her eyebrows bounced and one corner of her mouth popped up into a smile. "I run way too hot to be a robot."

An abrupt tightening of the muscles in Jeremy's hips made him shift in his seat. Isabel was going to make him crazy by the time this case was wrapped up. For once, Jeremy was glad for Mr. Summers's ridiculous timeline. The sooner this case was done, the sooner he could decide if he wanted to pursue anything with her. It seemed like he had to at least try one more time, leave her with a smile on her face rather than having her push him out the door. "I know that. Firsthand."

"I hope that doesn't make you uncomfortable. You know. That we slept together. I'm trying to look at it as an odd coincidence."

"So you definitely weren't spying on me and Mr. Summers in the bar at the Bacharach?"

Isabel's eyes went wide. "Is that who your meeting was with that night?" She clamped her hand over her mouth, much like she had when he'd mentioned that his new roommate, the stray cat with no name, was going to have kittens.

"It is. Summers loves the bar there."

Isabel reached out and clasped Jeremy's forearm.

"I swear I wasn't spying. I would never do that. I was legitimately up in my room trying to get some sleep when the silly alarm went off. It had been a hell of a day trying to find an apartment and look for a new office space. It's a lot to deal with at one time, especially when you're starting on a case that could easily end up being all-consuming."

Jeremy couldn't help but look at her hand on his arm, her slender fingers on the dark wool of his coat, and quietly wish he wasn't wearing a suit. "I had to ask." He cleared his throat, knowing he'd never truly believed that Isabel had been up to something nefarious that night, but it did make him wonder whether she was someone he could trust. "You know, I looked you up on the internet this afternoon. Judging by the work you were doing in DC, I'm up against quite a formidable foe."

"Please don't judge me by that. As far as I'm concerned, that was a lifetime ago. I'm actually getting ready to go into a whole new area of practice. Adoption law."

Now Jeremy was even more fascinated. This was a full one-eighty. "There's not exactly a lot of money in that, is there?"

Isabel shrugged. "There isn't. I'm not worried about that. I just want to have a body of work that I can be proud of."

"I take it that doesn't include the things you did in DC?"

She shook her head. "Definitely not. But I'm putting all of that behind me. For good."

So maybe he'd read Isabel all wrong. He could hardly fault a person for wanting to do some good with her career. "Sounds like you've got it all figured out."

"And speaking of getting things figured out, let's say we get the note authenticated. At that point, we'll need to set up a time for in-depth negotiations to hammer out the details. But I don't have an office right now."

Jeremy sucked in a deep breath. He had serious concerns that as soon as the note was deemed authentic, Mr. Summers would further dig in his heels. But it was part of Jeremy's job to at least move forward in good faith. "It's not easy for me to get much done at the Sharp and Sharp office. Too many interruptions." He cleared his throat, racking his brain for an idea. "Is meeting at Eden's an option?"

"They don't have the room. I asked about a work space there, but the building is old and they're bulging at the seams." She placed her napkin across her plate and sat back.

"I have a full office big enough for two people at my place in Brooklyn. In fact, I probably have too much space. I have meetings there all the time when I need quiet, or when a client wants more discretion than they'll get walking into the front door of a law firm. Would you be comfortable with that idea?"

"Hmm…" She squinted at him. "I don't know. Is this some sort of come-on?"

Jeremy could feel the heat rising in his cheeks. "Most women aren't seduced by the idea of negotiations."

"Ah, but I'm not most women."

Jeremy swallowed hard, finding it difficult to get past the lump in his throat. "I noticed."

Isabel granted him a small smile. "Would that mean I'd get to meet your cat?"

"She's not my cat."

"She's come up in conversation an awful lot for a cat that isn't yours."

"I'm not a cat person at all. I just took pity on her because she was outside in the cold. Ironically, the only reason I hadn't let her in before was because she was so fat. Now I know why."

"What are you going to do about the kittens?"

Jeremy kneaded his forehead. His meeting with his neighborhood veterinarian was still fresh in his mind. "For now? I'm fostering her. We had such a late summer that I guess there's a big surplus of cats and the shelters are full. The vet said the kittens should be ready for adoption by Valentine's Day." Jeremy could hardly believe the words out of his own mouth. Like he needed another complication in his life.

"Well, I can't wait to meet her. I love cats. We always had them when I was a kid. My mom was obsessed with them."

"You haven't had one since?"

Isabel's face reflected something Jeremy hadn't seen before—sadness. "No. Not one of my own."

"Well, good. Maybe you're the answer to my prayers. I'm a bit out of my depth." He glanced over at her, wondering why he was allowing himself to get further entwined with Isabel. He knew he shouldn't be, especially not now. He should be creating distance. That was how you won. "With the cat. Not the case."

Six

Isabel arranged to meet Mindy at her grandmother's penthouse apartment on Central Park West on Sunday morning. It was only eleven days until Christmas and the clock was ticking on Mr. Summers's timeline. The results of the promissory note authentication were due back tomorrow. Then Isabel would have to get back into it with Jeremy. She wasn't quite sure what to make of the invitation to meet at his house, but she knew from experience that there was no substitute for sitting down at the negotiating table and hammering out details. So she would risk having to endure the temptation of Jeremy, being alone and sequestered with him, just so she could move forward with her life—

finish up the Eden's case and start the new year with a whole new direction.

"Hey there." Mindy answered the door, dressed in the sort of outfit Isabel had never seen her wear—jeans and a sweater. No designer dress or sky-high heels. It was nice to see her dressed down and relaxed. "Come on in."

"Thanks." Isabel stepped into a bright and elegant foyer with white marble floors and a crystal-and-chrome fixture overhead. She took off her coat, glad she'd also gone for pants and a sweater. Even hot-running Isabel found it too cold outside for a dress.

"Thank you for suggesting we do this. It was a really good idea. Sophie is convinced that this whole Summers case is bogus. But I'm not so sure, especially after your forensic accountants found the money yesterday. And discovered that it went into my grandmother's personal account, not the business."

"It's starting to make sense now, isn't it? No wonder we couldn't find any evidence of it in the Eden's books. It never touched Eden's. Or at least not directly." Isabel was struggling just like Mindy, wondering how this all went together. "But we still don't know for certain that the money came from Summers and we also don't know where it eventually went."

"Only that it existed."

"Right."

Mindy waved Isabel across the foyer. "Come on. Let me show you the place."

They progressed down a skinny hallway and then the apartment opened up, with an entire wall of windows overlooking Central Park. The vista ahead was frosted with snow, a lovely match for the mostly white furnishings.

"My grandmother was all about punches of color." Mindy picked up a magenta throw pillow from one of several plush sofas. Behind it was a sunny yellow cashmere throw. The walls were dotted with an eclectic mix of art, wildly varied stylistically, from impressionist to modern, featuring nearly every shade of the rainbow. It all looked to be original. The space as a whole spoke of a very chic woman with impossibly expensive taste. Of course Victoria Eden had lived in such a grand and unbelievable space.

"I've seen that same thing at Eden's, especially in her old office."

Mindy nodded. "Emma's been afraid to change a thing. Too much tradition. The specter of my grandmother always looms large."

Tradition. Another reason Isabel could not let Eden's fall apart on her watch.

"I can't believe you never moved in here," Isabel said. "It's incredible. Completely gorgeous." She wandered over to a set of French doors that led out to a stone balcony, admiring the wintry scene. Mother Nature had already gone big this December.

"I knew that no matter what I did, Sophie would criticize my choices unless I left everything exactly as it was. And I do not want to live in a museum."

"That's not really fair to you, is it? So you just leave this sitting here because of your sister?"

Mindy shrugged. "I have no business complaining. Emma never knew our grandmother very well, so she enjoys coming up here and poking around, looking at old photos. Sophie likes it for the same reason, and I'd be lying if I said that I didn't enjoy it, too. It's comforting to be here. I can feel our grandmother's presence when I'm here and we all miss it. I can't fault anyone for wanting to put the world on pause."

Isabel nodded, appreciating the whole sad story. She knew very well what it was like to miss someone so desperately. She still felt that same way about her parents, especially her mom. "If only we could do that. It would be nice every now and then."

Mindy gathered her glorious red tresses in her hands and draped them over one shoulder. "It's only been a year since Gram died, and so much has happened. Just when we thought we were getting the store back on a more profitable path, this happens. I'm honestly wondering if we're not better off just selling, paying off Mr. Summers and moving on. I know Sophie and Emma want to keep Eden's alive at any cost, but sometimes, things just don't work out."

Isabel carefully considered Mindy's words. She loved that her future sister-in-law was both savvy and sweet. She could make shrewd business moves and still take everyone's feelings into account. "Have

I told you how happy I am that my brother found a woman who is not only smart, but also incredibly thoughtful?"

Mindy smiled. "That's not what you thought of me the first time we met."

"I know. And I fully admit that you changed my mind."

Mindy reached out and rubbed Isabel's arm. "I'm excited to have you for a sister-in-law. Although, honestly, I have a feeling that I should probably just call you my sister. You and I are a lot more alike than Sophie or Emma and I."

Isabel felt like her heart was growing to twice its normal size. She and Sam were impossibly close, but that was such a small circle of family. Here was Mindy, forging a connection of her own with Isabel. She was so thankful for it. "That sounds amazing. I've always wanted a sister."

"Consider it done." Mindy grinned and placed her arm around Isabel's shoulders, pulling her close. "Come on. Let's go dig through my grandmother's office."

The pair trekked through the living room to what appeared to be Victoria Eden's private quarters, with a large master bedroom, elegant bathroom with its own view of the park, dressing room and, finally, a generous home office. Like the rest of the house, a neutral backdrop of white and cream made room for the more over-the-top elements, like a crimson velvet club chair. Mindy stepped behind her grandmother's grand desk and opened the closet to reveal six large filing cabinets.

"I'm guessing we start here?" Mindy asked.

Isabel didn't have a better suggestion. "It's as good a place as any."

They quickly set up a system, methodically going through one drawer at a time, file folder after file folder, page after page of surprisingly meaningless paperwork. For a woman who had been considered a business tycoon, Victoria Eden had been keenly focused on the smallest of things.

Mindy shook her head and closed one folder. "She kept nearly thirty years of electric bills. Who does that?"

"Someone who's watching every penny? Maybe that's part of why she was so successful."

Mindy's shoulders dropped in exasperation. "I hope this doesn't end up being a big waste of time."

"I don't know. Compared to most things I do, this is pretty fun. Plus, we get to spend time together."

"There you go. Good job looking on the bright side. I need to do more of that."

"Actually, if anything, I'd take all of this mundane stuff as a good sign. Anyone who kept electric bills likely also kept far more important things."

"Even superpersonal things?"

Isabel closed up the folder she'd been sifting through and handed it over to Mindy. "Especially that."

After two more hours of pulling apart the contents of the filing cabinets, they were down to the last drawer. Mindy pulled the handle, but it only opened partway. "Can you help me with this?" she asked, peering down inside.

Isabel rushed over and knelt down next to Mindy. Sure enough, there was a large wood box, turned on its side, preventing the drawer from being opened the whole way. Mindy and Isabel quickly pulled out the hanging files in front of it. Mindy grabbed a letter opener from her grandmother's desk drawer and slipped it under the bottom of the box, twisting and pulling until the box popped free with a clatter of wood against metal.

Mindy closed the drawer and sat spread-eagled on the floor with the box between her knees. She flipped the small brass latch on the front. She looked up at Isabel, her eyes wide with astonishment. "It's a bunch of letters." She examined the first envelope. "The return address says Bradley Summers."

Goose bumps popped up on Isabel's arms. She sensed that another piece of the puzzle was about to fall into place. "Bingo."

Isabel and Mindy spent the next several hours devouring the correspondence sent by Bradley Summers to Victoria Eden, which seemed to begin in the spring of 1979, years before the loan would have been made. They arranged the letters in chronological order, which helped them sort out how the affair began: after Bradley and Victoria had a chance meeting at a cocktail party in the Hamptons. Bradley made mention that he was glad their spouses had not been on hand—Bradley's wife because she'd had one of her "many migraines" and Victoria's husband because he couldn't be bothered to stay away from the racetrack. It was an epic love story that sprouted up between two people thrown together by chance, who just happened to fulfill what the other was so desperately looking for. For the senior Mr. Summers, it seemed to be the undivided attention of a woman. *My sweet Victoria*, he wrote, *When we're together, I feel like I'm the only man in the world. Every moment with you is priceless, worth framing and hanging in a museum.*

"Wow. This is so romantic. They were head over heels for each other," Isabel said, handing over the letter she was holding to Mindy. She couldn't help but be astonished by what had been between these two people, sentiments that served as a very plain reminder that Isabel hadn't come close to finding that kind of passion or affection with a man. She hoped she wasn't running out of time.

When Mindy finished reading the final letter in the box, she looked over at Isabel with a tear in her eye. It was a bit incongruous with Mindy's normally tough exterior. "Their love affair was real." Mindy's shoulders dropped. "I don't know what to think about this. Or how I'm supposed to feel. I really loved my grandfather, but it's pretty well known in our family that he was not a great husband. This is at least confirmation that my grandmother stayed in a loveless marriage for her entire life."

"That part is incredibly sad." Isabel glanced down at the pile of letters. "It was also pretty clear that your grandfather had a serious gambling problem. Bradley mentions several times that he hated your grandmother living with the burden of his many debts. Do you think that's where the money could have gone?"

Mindy shrugged. "I have no idea. I mean, going to the racetrack with our grandfather is one of the only things I ever remember doing with him, but we were kids and it was nothing but fun. We'd drink soda and eat junk food and he'd let us pick our favorite horses so he could place bets. Sophie always picked names like Fancy Frolic, and I always picked ones like Emperor King. My grandfather used to tease me, saying that I needed to learn to like 'girl things.'" Mindy made air quotes. "As far as I was concerned, I liked what I liked. No big surprise, but he handed those same ideas down to our dad. Even so, those days at the track are some of my fondest memories of my grandfather. He at least wanted to spend time with us, which is more than I can say for my dad."

Isabel was struck by how even a family with great wealth and power could have such a bittersweet legacy. "If the money went to gambling debts, it might be harder to track down, especially depending on who he owed money to. And it still doesn't change the fact that it appears that the loan was real."

Mindy again looked down at the letters in her hand, but it was for several moments this time. She brushed her fingers across the envelope at the top of the pile. "This means that the store is really on the line, doesn't it? We aren't talking hypotheticals anymore. I mean, chances are that the promissory note is real, and we're going to have to find a way to pay off the debt."

"No matter what I'm able to negotiate, chances are that it'll still be a huge chunk of money, and from everything I've seen of Mr. Summers, he's serious about wanting it in one lump sum, right away. Early January, right after New Year's."

"It's just hard to come up with that kind of cash without a loan. And the most valuable thing we have to use as collateral is Eden's. It's all Sophie has, aside from her apartment and Eden House, our family's vacation home, which she would never let go of in a million years."

"What about selling this apartment?"

Mindy nodded, looking around the room. "Yeah. I could definitely do that, but we're talking maybe fifty million, and that's if we get top dollar from the right buyer, which could easily take a year to happen. It's a drop in the bucket compared to what we have to come up with."

"Can Sam help?"

"He's looking into selling some bigger properties, but like I said, that all takes time, and it all costs money, too. Real estate agents need to get paid. It sort of feels like we're throwing money into a big black hole." Surprisingly, a smile crossed Mindy's face.

"And you're happy about that?"

"No. No. I was just thinking about Sam and his reaction to this whole situation. He wants to fix everything. He gets so worked up about it, wanting to hold everything together. It's just so damn sweet. Every time he gets upset about it, I fall a little more in love with him."

Now Isabel was the one having to fight back tears. The struggles she and Sam had been through when they were young had been much harder on him, and Isabel still had a good deal of guilt over having been away at college when it happened. "You really love him, don't you?"

"It might sound corny, and I'm not a super sentimental person, but he is my soul mate. We work together in every way. I can't imagine my life without him." Mindy gathered the letters in her hands and squared the edges on the floor. "And I nearly lost him. I pushed him away so many times."

Isabel had never pushed anyone away, but she'd had many men shutter her out of their lives. It hurt an unimaginable amount, which was a big part of the reason Isabel had not initially liked Mindy. She hated the thought of her brother having his heart broken. "I feel like everything happens for a reason. Maybe you had to go through those early tests to know for sure that you're right for each other."

"That sounds a lot nicer than my version, which is basically just me being an idiot." Mindy shifted to her knees and got up from the floor. "So what do you think is going to happen with Eden's?"

"I think we're going to have to count on Mr. Summers's good graces and hope that they'll agree to a reduced settlement and a payment plan."

"Do you think these letters might help?" Mindy asked. "What if we showed them to him? Showed him how much his father really loved my grandmother? It might make him see that the loan really was made out of love. It's not our fault his parents couldn't make their marriage work."

Isabel shook her head. "No. Absolutely not. I think you should put those letters back where you found them, and for the time being, I wouldn't tell anyone about them other than Sam and your sisters."

"Okay, then. What's next?"

"I'm guessing that I'm going to get a phone call from Jeremy Sharp tomorrow morning saying that the note was authenticated. And that's when we start negotiating from a disadvantage."

"You don't think you're better than him?"

Now it was Isabel's turn to smile at an inopportune time. "It's not a matter of better. Jeremy is plenty skilled. He's a shrewd attorney."

Mindy narrowed her sights, and Isabel immediately worried that her future sister-in-law was onto something. "Is it just me or is he superhot, too? I mean, I know Sam thinks he's a weasel, but there's no accounting for his taste. Especially not when it comes to hotness."

Isabel's cheeks flushed with warmth. There had been many times at dinner the other night when she'd caught herself holding her breath in awe of Jeremy's appeal. "He's extremely handsome. There's no doubt about that."

"It was sexy the way you two were arguing at that first meeting. It felt like there were sparks flying. Or is that stupid of me to say?"

Isabel already felt bad about not coming clean about Jeremy with her own brother the day of that meeting. She wasn't sure she could keep it from Mindy, too, especially when they were becoming so close. "I have to tell you something. But you have to promise not to breathe a word of it to Sam. At least not until the case is settled." She bit down on her lip, waiting for Mindy's response, hoping like hell that she could truly be trusted.

"I don't like the idea of secrets. But I also don't like the idea of you feeling like you can't tell me any-thing. Because you can." Mindy nodded eagerly. "So, yes. My lips are zipped. I won't say a peep to Sam."

Isabel took in a deep breath for confidence. "I slept with Jeremy."

Mindy slugged her in the arm playfully. "Shut up. Are you serious?" Her eyes bugged out. "Wait. When?"

"It was actually a few days before the first meet-ing. I had no idea who he was, and he had no idea who I was. It was pure coincidence." Isabel went on to share the most general of details from their night together, sparing Mindy the part about Jeremy's quick departure.

"So, how was it?"

"It was fantastic, but it was a one-night thing. You don't have anything to worry about. There will be no conflict of interest there. Jeremy's all business and he's devoted to his client. That goes much further than you might imagine."

"I trust your judgment, Isabel. Completely. I know you're an amazing lawyer and I'm sure you won't have a problem keeping it all aboveboard. So, how do you like our odds of saving the store?"

Isabel didn't want to sugarcoat anything, but she didn't want to set her future sister-in-law up for disappointment, either. "The optimist in me is thinking fifty-fifty."

"Really?" Mindy asked. "That bad?"

Isabel reached out and caressed Mindy's arm, wanting to be at least a little reassuring. "I'm going to do everything I can to keep you from losing."

"Everything?" Mindy asked with two perfectly arched eyebrows.

Isabel was now second-guessing the decision to spill the beans about Jeremy. She really hoped she didn't end up regretting it. "Nearly everything."

Mindy and Isabel put away the letters, tidied up the office, and went their separate ways. It was a chilly day, but the sun had come out, so Isabel decided to walk back to the Bacharach. When she arrived, there was a sign on the door: *All guests: Please see the front desk for information regarding your stay. There will be no new check-ins until further notice.*

Isabel strode inside to investigate, but there was a sizable line of seemingly upset guests at the front desk. "What's going on?" she asked a woman who was waiting for the elevator.

"The fire department has ordered the hotel to replace the alarm system. They start the work on Friday. Everyone has to be out by then." The elevator dinged. "It doesn't affect me, so I'm not too worried about it."

Isabel decided she wasn't going to wait with the angry mob in the lobby and instead took the elevator up with the woman. "Did they happen to say if they're sending guests to another hotel?"

"It's Christmas in Manhattan. There are no other hotel rooms. That's why everyone is so mad."

Isabel wasn't sure how things could get much worse. She'd just have to move in with Sam and Mindy for a few days until she could find something more permanent. If nothing else, she needed to get back to looking for an apartment in earnest.

The woman got off on her floor and Isabel rode up another two to her own. She'd hardly keyed her way into her room when her phone rang. It was Jeremy.

"Hello?" she asked, plopping down on the bed.

"Did I catch you at a bad time?"

Isabel disliked the way her body reacted to his voice, like a puppy that's just been told it's time for a treat. "No. It's fine. What's up?"

"We got the authentication of the note. I just wanted to tell you as soon as I knew."

Isabel reclined back on the bed and stared up at the ceiling. This was not surprising news, but it was certainly not what they wanted. "Okay, then. I'll notify my client. And I guess we need to get together to hammer out these negotiations."

"Yeah. About that. I talked to Mr. Summers and in light of the authentication, he has changed his terms. He wants an even billion or the store. By January 1."

She shot straight up in bed, her heart hammering. She could hardly believe what he had just said. "It's Christmas. Is he really that cold and heartless? I'm sorry, but your client is behaving like Ebenezer Scrooge."

"From where I'm sitting, he has an ironclad case."

Isabel fought the grumble in her throat. She also tamped back her natural urge to launch into her side of the argument. There was no point in that right now. Isabel had seen the letters. She'd known that this was coming. Victoria Eden and Bradley Summers had absolutely had an affair. And by all accounts, it had been a doozy. Her heart sank at the thought of the call she had to make, to break this news to Mindy and Sam, then let them break it to Sophie and Emma. It would take the wind out of their sails, for sure, but Isabel would not let this be the end of the story. It would not be the final chapter of Eden's Department Store. Somehow, they would pull this off. She would. "I'll talk to my clients and see what we can do."

"You'll get back to me?"

"I don't see that I have a choice."

Seven

Since the moment the promissory note had been authenticated, Isabel had been doing nothing but playing cat and mouse with Jeremy. His client was refusing to budge. Mr. Summers wouldn't give an inch. Jeremy was holding fast. She knew from experience that she'd never be able to exercise any influence over him unless they could meet in person, but he was insisting on phone calls, much to her dismay. He was avoiding her, and it was starting to feel personal.

By Friday, things were becoming dire. Sam and Mindy had spent the entire week moving assets, trying to sell properties, but they were finding the task more difficult the closer they got to the holidays. It would be nearly impossible to liquidate anything between Christmas and New Year's. There were simply too many people who weren't working. With Christmas six days away, time was running out.

As if life couldn't possibly get more complicated, Isabel had to vacate the Bacharach by noon that day. She'd originally planned to stay with Sam and Mindy, but they'd both been working so hard that they'd managed to come down with a dreadful cold. Isabel's back-up plan was to fly to DC and stay with a friend for the weekend. This close to Christmas, there wasn't a spare hotel room anywhere in the city.

Before she left for the airport, Isabel was set to meet with Sophie and Emma at Eden's and if all went okay, Sam or Mindy would call in. Isabel arrived at Eden's first thing that morning. Eight o'clock to be exact, right when the offices were first open. A burly but friendly security officer named Duane met her at one of the main entrances.

"Sophie and Emma are already here," he said, walking her through the cosmetics department and back to the executive elevators.

"Thank you. Have they been here long?"

"Most of the night."

Isabel had been afraid of that. Coming up with a cool billion to get Benjamin Summers to go away was no small job and they were all going to extraordinary measures to attempt the impossible.

The store was eerily quiet, with only a handful of lights on. It would open early at 9:00 a.m. for holiday shopping hours, but there was still a sense that she was taking part in a death march. Just like the entire Eden family, she desperately didn't want the store to slip into Mr. Summers's hands. There were no guarantees that he'd continue to run the store at all. Isabel could imagine him taking a wrecking ball to the whole thing out of spite. What would happen to the employees? Or the history contained in this beautiful old building? And what would happen to the Eden sisters if they lost their birthright, this very permanent fixture of this city, emblazoned with their name?

Duane pressed the elevator button for her. "Do you know your way upstairs? Lizzie, the receptionist, should be here soon, but not yet. She just texted me to say her train was delayed."

"Eden's really is like a family, isn't it?" Isabel asked. Where else did the receptionist check in with the security guard when she was running late?

"Yes, ma'am. Lizzie is like a little sister to me. She tells me everything." His eyebrows bounced and he smiled. "Even about her new beau."

"Ooh. Anyone I know?" Lizzie was a total sweetheart and Isabel had grown to adore her.

"I shouldn't say anything." Duane's face said that he was dying to tell someone.

Isabel reached out and touched his arm. "Look. I'm very good at keeping secrets. You can tell me. I won't say a peep."

"It's James, one of the salespeople in menswear," he blurted. "He's a Brit like Emma's husband, Daniel."

As if there hadn't been enough excitement about the Eden family, Emma and Daniel had decided to get married at city hall last week. With a baby on the way, Daniel was eager to start the process of becoming an American citizen, apparently much to his mother's disappointment.

"I'll have to find a reason to sneak down to menswear later and see if I can get an eyeful of James."

Duane laughed and the elevator dinged. "Have a good meeting."

"Thank you." A minute later, Isabel arrived on the executive floor.

Sophie was waiting right outside the elevator bank, pacing. She lunged for Isabel the instant the door opened. "Thank God you're here. We have an emergency and it's bad."

Isabel could hardly keep up anymore. She'd dealt with plenty of panicked clients, but this was turning into an hourly thing with the Eden family. Fortunately, she had a great deal of experience in this arena. "Whatever it is, it's okay. Did something happen with one of the deals Sam and Mindy were working on? Or something you and your husband were setting up?"

Emma strode out of her office. Her baby bump was now visible. Small, but apparent. "I read the article, Sophie. I really don't think it's that bad. I mean, it's not great, but I've seen worse things."

Isabel was starting to put this all together. "Something in the tabloids, I take it?"

Sophie waved her ahead. "Come on. My office. I'll show you."

Isabel was starting to bristle at Sophie's cloak-and-dagger approach as she found herself marching with Sophie and Emma down the hall to Sophie's office. Inside, a stack of newspapers sat on her desk. Even upside down, Isabel saw the headline: Eden's Matriarch's Secret Affair Exposed. Of course, those words—*secret affair*—leaped off the page. Isabel wasn't much for prurient accounts, but anyone would have to be intrigued. "How did this happen?" Isabel took the liberty of taking a copy and began scanning the story.

"We have no idea. I guess the reporter called Mindy last night but she was so hopped up on cold medicine that she barely remembers the conversation."

Isabel had to hand it to Mindy. For someone on cold medicine, the quote she'd given the newspaper was remarkably smart and diplomatic. She'd said precisely what Isabel would have coached her to say. Mr. Summers, however, was a different case. Clearly Jeremy had *not* had a say in the formulation of his comment. No lawyer would have allowed their client to say such a thing.

"It's so horrible. The things he said about our grandmother." Sophie plopped down on the couch. "And right before Christmas, no less. I wouldn't be surprised if people start boycotting the store. We need to hire a PR person and start fighting this. We need to put our own version of this story out there. We can't let Gram's memory be tarnished like this."

Isabel very pointedly shook her head at Emma, who was the only one paying attention to her. Sophie was dead wrong. "Actually, ladies, this is amazing news. I believe we finally have a leg up in this negotiation."

Jeremy had reached a new low—he arrived at the office having had no more than ten minutes of sleep. Granted, it was Friday morning and it had been an incredibly long week, which usually left him stumbling into the weekend. With his grueling job, he already didn't sleep well. but that had gotten progressively worse since his night with Isabel. She was this beautiful dangling string in his life, unfinished business, both personally and professionally. Situations like that had always bothered him.

When Kelsey left him, it was yet another situation where he was left with far more questions than answers. She took off with no warning, leaving only a note that he'd made her deeply unhappy. He never had the chance to ask how or why—she went right to the press and smeared him, telling them their marriage was over. It wasn't until later that Jeremy learned she'd been unfaithful, but he couldn't prove it, and the court of public opinion was squarely against him. He'd been painted as heartless, and since it was clear to Jeremy that the situation would not get better if he spoke up, he put his head down and gave in to her demands. Just to get her out of his life. He simply hadn't had the fight.

If Jeremy had learned anything over the past five days, it was that the Eden family would go down swinging. Isabel had been incredible to work with, and they'd talked every day, but she was doing nothing but push, even from her disadvantaged position. He loved the fight in her. He loved it a little too much. Every conversation with her was a turn-on, precisely why he'd made excuses all week and kept their back-and-forth on the phone.

Of course, last night before he left the office, Isabel had called him on it. "I'm beginning to think you're avoiding me, Sharp." She referred to him by his last name when she really wanted to put on the pressure. It was playful and toying and sexy. On some level, she *had* to know what it was doing to him. "Why don't we meet for a drink? Or I'll come out to Brooklyn. I still haven't met your cat. Does she have a name yet?"

"I'm calling her Cat."

"You have got to be kidding me."

Jeremy had not appreciated the inference. "No. I am a kind soul who took in an animal. But she's not staying and I don't want to get attached. Hence, I put only enough time into giving her a name as absolutely necessary. Her next owner can give her a real name."

"Any sign of the kittens?"

"Soon, I guess."

"You guess?" Isabel then went on to read him a laundry list of the things he should be looking for in Cat's behavior. He had noticed nothing she mentioned.

Jeremy's only response had been to change the subject. "My client refuses to budge, so unless you have a check for me to collect, I guess I don't see the point in a face-to-face meeting."

"I think that what you're really saying is that it's harder to negotiate with me when you and I are in the same room."

She was *not* wrong. In fact, that had been his number one fear—Isabel would get him to do something he shouldn't if they had to meet in person. Sure, he *wanted* to see her. He'd be an idiot to not want that. But was it a good idea? No. "Goodbye, Ms. Blackwell. Have a good night."

Jeremy had called Mr. Summers immediately after, but got nowhere. "There is no wiggle room," Mr. Summers said. "From where I sit, we have them right where we want them. They will pay or they'll hand over the store. They're lying and stalling."

"Every day they continue to delay is another day you have to pay me. We could expedite the process and get it all wrapped up if you were willing to concede to a payment plan. You'll still get your money, just on a different timeline."

"No. Absolutely not. And please don't ask me again."

Jeremy had a duty to give Mr. Summers whatever he wanted, no matter how punitive he was being about the whole thing. "Very well then. Have a good night."

Now back at work, he couldn't get his head screwed on right. Maybe Isabel was right. Maybe they did need to meet. He couldn't concede with anything, but he could at least see her. Let her beat him up with her words. It would likely be the only fun to be had with this case.

"Knock, knock." Jeremy's father appeared at his office door. "Good morning."

Simply hearing his father's voice these days made him cringe, and this reaction was starting to get to him. He didn't enjoy having this negative relationship. In fact, he hated it. His only real hope was to keep plugging ahead so that he could convince his dad to retire or at least taper down to far fewer hours in the office. Once they could lessen the day-to-day professional grind that was ever-present between them, Jeremy hoped they could return to being what they should be—father and son. "Hey. Good morning."

His dad took a seat on the leather sofa just inside the door of Jeremy's office. "I need to steal you for a few minutes. I spoke with Benjamin Summers on my way in."

Jeremy didn't need to hear another word to know that this was likely bad. "Why did he call you? I always make myself available to him. Always."

"He didn't. I called him."

Jeremy instantly found his hands balling up into fists. His neck went tight. His jaw, too. "He's my client. Why would you do that?"

"I'm seeing no movement on this case, Jeremy. I had to know that he was happy."

"Then ask me directly. I would've gotten you up to speed without you making me look bad to a client." Jeremy leaned forward in his chair and planted his elbow on his desk, closing his eyes and attempting to knead away the tension in his forehead with his hand. But the more he thought about it, the angrier he became. Finally, he pushed back from his desk and stood, marching over to his dad with determination. He wanted him to know that this was serious. He would not let this stand. "In fact, I'd say that what you did was wholly unprofessional. You don't just make me look bad, you make the entire firm look bad. And there's absolutely no reason for it other than the fact that you don't trust me to do what I need to do."

"I trusted you with the Patterson case. We all know how that ended."

"I was in the middle of getting a divorce and my soon-to-be ex-wife, who I thought loved me, was dragging my name through the tabloids. If I wasn't on top of my game at the time, I think it's understandable."

"You can't allow your personal life to get in the way of your job."

"And I might have let that happen one time, but

it's not the case right now. Summers isn't budging on anything, and Eden's simply doesn't have the capital to pay him off in a single lump-sum cash payment, as he's demanding."

"Sometimes, it's a lawyer's job to convince a client that it's in their best interest to move the goalposts."

"I understand that. And I have tried. It's only been a few weeks. The trouble is that what I really think he wants is revenge. And I don't think that's possible."

His dad drew a deep breath through his nose, looking right at Jeremy, although in many ways it felt as though he was looking through him. Jeremy never felt that his dad truly saw him. "I just want you to get this done. Get together with Ms. Blackwell and remind her in person that she has no choice but to acquiesce to Summers's demands. I'm not buying that they don't have the cash. The Edens' war chest has to run deep."

Jeremy nodded. "I'll get it done. But it's not because you decided to interfere. I have it under control. I wish you knew that."

His dad stood, which was a great relief to Jeremy. Hopefully this meant he was leaving. "I don't care what it takes. Lock yourselves up in a room until there's only one person left standing."

Jeremy fought back a grin, which at least helped the tightness in his neck go away. How he would love a negotiation with Isabel that involved them locked away. The tougher she proved herself to be, the more he wanted to show her that he could match her intensity. In every way. "I'll suggest it."

"And another thing, you need to be careful with this Blackwell woman. I looked into her history and she's worked with some very high-level but shady clients. There's no telling what she'll pull to make Summers go away. We should be ready to torpedo her in the press if necessary."

Jeremy took a step forward. "Dad. No." Even he was surprised at his protective response. He might not know Isabel very well, but he didn't want his dad to go after her. Not like that. As someone who'd been taken down by the tabloids, Jeremy knew firsthand exactly how brutal it was. He didn't want that for anyone. Jeremy wasn't going to fault Isabel for the things she'd had to do professionally. He knew very well how lawyers could get pushed into a corner by a client and have no real choice but to work their way out. It was how you got ahead. It was how you made a name for yourself. "We're not doing that. It's unseemly and unnecessary."

"You're too soft, Jeremy. Always have been. You let Kelsey walk all over you. You're letting Summers do it to you, too."

I loved Kelsey. And I'm trying to make my client happy. "I'll get it done without torpedoing anyone. I will get both sides to meet somewhere in the middle."

His dad pursed his lips, a sign that he remained unconvinced. "It'd better be a lot closer to what Summers wants than the middle."

"It will be."

His dad turned to leave. No handshake. No pat on the shoulder. Just one lawyer leaving another lawyer's office. But he stopped when he reached the doorway. "Have you and your mother talked about the tree-trimming party?"

Christmas. Jeremy was so knee-deep in this case, his mother was the only thing reminding him that the holiday was just around the corner. "We did. A few days ago. Although there's not much to talk about, is there? We've been doing this every year on December 23 for as long as I can remember."

"And it's my job as your father to make sure you're going to be there. You're the only child and your mom looks forward to that night all year long."

"I will not disappoint her."

Jeremy's dad had hardly been gone a minute before Jeremy's phone rang. His heart sped up when he saw the caller ID. It was Isabel. "Hey there. Calling to give me a hard time about the cat again?"

"Have you seen the papers?" Isabel's voice could sometimes be cutting, but her tone was particularly icy.

"I haven't. I never read them."

"I suggest you do it right now. You can look on-line. Do a search for Eden's Department Store. I'm sure it'll come right up."

Jeremy took a seat at his desk. "Can I call you back when I'm done?"

"I'd rather wait on the line and hear your reaction."

This couldn't be good. "Ten minutes. I'll call you back. I promise." He ended the call and did exactly what she suggested. When the headline popped up in the search results, Jeremy's stomach sank so low it felt like it was at his knees. The words "secret affair" jumped right out at him.

Jeremy only had time to scan the article. He wanted to call Mr. Summers before he spoke to Isabel and he knew she'd hold him to the promise of ten minutes. The story laid out the facts as the two parties generally understood them. The bad of it was that these details had now become public information. The worst of it was the comments from Mr. Summers as contrasted with those from Mindy Eden. Mindy's only comment was, "Mr. Summers has made a claim and we're doing everything we can to negotiate with him in good faith. My sisters and I loved our grandmother very much and want everyone to know that she was a generous and kind person with a big heart."

Mr. Summers's comment wasn't quite so delicate. "Victoria Eden barged into my parents' marriage and destroyed it. She was a vile money-hungry woman who handed her naive granddaughters a business wrongly built on my father's money. I will get restitution if it's the last thing I do."

Jeremy physically winced when he reread it. Then he picked up the phone and called his client. "Mr. Summers. I saw your quote in the newspaper today. You have painted us into a corner."

"That reporter misquoted me."

"You might have to prove that to me. Do you know who fed the story to the papers in the first place?"

"I don't."

Jeremy wasn't convinced, but he had no evidence that his client had started this. "Okay, then. I'm calling to let you know that the Eden's team has read the article and they are not happy about the things you said. They could easily countersue you for defamation of character."

"You can't defame the dead. I looked it up."

"Ah, but survivors can make a claim that the defamation of their dead relative reflects on their reputation. Knowing Ms. Blackwell's previous legal work, I have no doubt she will make exactly that argument." Jeremy took in a deep breath and kept going. "Also, the Eden sisters are immensely popular in the city of New York. They are in the tabloids all the time. People love them and their store. So if you think that you could somehow get somewhere by bad-mouthing them to the press, you were sorely mistaken. Public opinion is important, Ben. And you have officially hurt your own chances by trying to mess with the Eden heiresses."

Mr. Summers cleared his throat. "What do you suggest I do? Call the reporter?"

"What's done is done. Nobody reads retractions, anyway. I want you to give me permission to negotiate with Eden's. You're going to have to give a little."

A distinct grumble came from the other end of the line. "Promise me you'll give up as little as possible."

"I'll do my best." Jeremy said goodbye and hung up, wasting no time returning Isabel's call. "I'm sorry," he said when she answered. "I saw the article. He claims he was misquoted, but regardless, people are reading it and I'm sorry that it happened in the first place. We need to get this hashed out."

"I can't negotiate with you if you won't give in on anything, Sharp."

He caught himself smiling. How could she do that when he was as stressed as could be? "Will you please stop calling me that? You've seen me naked. Can we go with Jeremy?"

"Are we starting negotiations already? Because I think you know that you're now the one at a disadvantage. Which means that technically, I can probably call you whatever I want."

Jeremy sat back in his chair and glanced out the window. It was starting to snow. He was tired. He really just wanted to get home. "If you're going to call me something bad, I think you should say it to my face."

"Oh, so now you'll meet with me in person? Now that you're forced to do it? That doesn't say much about your good faith, Jeremy."

Good God, it made heat rush through him to hear her say his first name. Inviting her to his place was not a great idea. But he had to get this done, get his dad and Mr. Summers off his back, and well, there was the matter of Cat, too. Isabel seemed to know what she was talking about when it came to his feline houseguest. "I know. I know. You were right all along. I owed you this meeting days ago. You can come to Brooklyn and meet Cat and we'll get things worked out."

"Actually, I was about to get on a plane back to DC. I've been kicked out of my hotel for the weekend and there are no vacancies this close to Christmas. My brother and Mindy both have some dreadful cold, so I don't want to stay with them. I can't afford to get sick."

Jeremy's mind was racing. He had more than enough room for Isabel. But could he resist her for a night or two? "I could put you up. If it's just for the weekend. In your own room, of course."

"You have that kind of space at your place?"

Jeremy wanted to keep things simple. He wasn't about to explain to Isabel that he had a big empty house because he'd been stupid enough to hope that someday he and his wife would have children. "I do. Plenty of room."

"Okay, then. Text me the address and I'll be there a little after noon, suitcase in hand."

Eight

Isabel had no idea what to expect when she got out of the car in front of Jeremy's brownstone. Overhead, the early-afternoon sky had darkened with clouds and big, fat flakes were falling steadily. Ahead, an ornate wrought iron gate awaited, with a long flight of stairs up to a beautiful arched wood door. It was straight out of a movie, but Isabel couldn't help but notice that Jeremy's neighbors all had Christmas wreaths or holiday garland adorning their facade. Not Jeremy. Not the guy who couldn't be bothered to give a cat a proper name. Which was just fine with Isabel. It wasn't like she was doing much better with celebrating the holiday.

She rang the bell and waited for Jeremy to answer.

When he unlatched the lock and opened the door, she was presented with an image she admired a little too much—Jeremy with his salt-and-pepper temples wearing a black sweater and dark jeans. "You weren't kidding about the suitcase." He gestured with a nod.

"I never joke about imposing on someone for a night or two. Are you sure this is okay? Are you sure you have enough room?"

Jeremy rolled his eyes and reached for her bag. "I wouldn't extend the invitation if I didn't have the space. I've put up plenty of clients at the house."

"But never opposing counsel, I'm guessing." Isabel followed him inside, where a square of beautifully restored ebony penny-tile floor marked the landing. From this first peek, his home was a showplace, every detail exceptional. Above, the ceiling soared with graceful moldings, lit up by vintage fixtures of seeded glass and rich bronze. To her left, a staircase with neat white treads and a scrolled black railing led to the floor above, then doubled back, climbing to yet another level. Ahead, a glossy dark wood floor stretched the full length of the house, past what appeared to be living room and kitchen, ending when it reached tall leaded windows through which she saw only snow-dusted trees. Taking this all in felt like more than a view of Jeremy's residence. It felt like a look into his soul. For the man who seemed to bristle at any personal burden, keeping this home had to be, on some level, a labor of love.

He closed the door behind her, set down her bag

and came up beside her, giving her a whiff of his irresistible smell. It was like the finest bourbon, rich and warm without any trace of booziness. "Actually, you'd be wrong about that. I did a negotiation here when another lawyer had a long layover at JFK. His flight got canceled and he ended up spending the night."

Isabel felt a little better about the propriety of this now. Although given her history with Jeremy, their situation wasn't *exactly* the same. "I see."

"No need to be jealous," Jeremy said. "He wasn't anywhere near as cute as you."

Isabel blushed and smiled, but then a spark in his eye caught her gaze and she was immobilized by the zap of electricity only Jeremy could deliver. Mere inches separated them, reminding her body of how blissful it was to be pressed against him, comb her fingers through his thick hair and kiss him. The fact that he was tossing around words like *cute* wasn't making him any easier to resist.

"I hate that it's this close to Christmas and we have to do this," he said, leaning against the stair railing.

"As far as I'm concerned, as long as the fire alarm doesn't go off, this is a vacation."

"Brooklyn *is* lovely this time of year." It was Jeremy's turn to smile, but that only made her want him more. She was going to have to learn to ignore the four or five hundred irresistible traits he seemed to have. Too bad she needed the negotiations ahead to go smoothly. A little jerkish behavior on his part might help stem her personal tide of desire.

Isabel laughed. "It's fine. I don't celebrate Christmas anyway."

"Jewish?"

She shook her head. "No. Just a habit I got into a long time ago."

He pressed his lips together and nodded. "Come on. I'll show you the place."

Jeremy provided a quick tour of the main floor—a comfortable living room with chocolate-brown leather furniture in front of a stately fireplace with a carved white stone surround that had to be an antique. The kitchen was a cook's delight with a generous center island topped with Carrara marble and custom cabinets of creamy gray. The sink overlooked a courtyard off the back of the house, with a patio shielded from the outside world by a row of snow-flocked Italian cypress trees, the kind you see growing alongside the roads of Tuscany.

Isabel went to the window to admire Jeremy's outdoor retreat, an uncommon luxury, even in Brooklyn. "It's so lovely out there. It must be amazing to sit out there in the spring or summer with a book."

Jeremy came right up behind her and Isabel stayed impossibly still, keenly aware of her breaths as they filled her lungs. This house was a magical place, an oasis of calm and beauty in the middle of a bustling metropolis, and its owner a little too enticing. "Actually, it's even better in the fall, when there's a nip of cold in the air. I get the firepit going and can sit outside for hours."

That sounded like sheer heaven to Isabel. "The house is beautiful. Truly stunning." She dared to turn around and face him. In the natural light coming from the window, he was somehow even more handsome. More kissable.

"Thank you. It was a big project. It did not look like this when we bought it."

We, meaning he and his wife. She really didn't want Jeremy to know that she'd gone digging into his private history, so she kept that detail to herself. "Oh?"

He stuffed his hands into his pockets and cast his sights down at the floor. "Yeah. I was married until a few years ago. She really wanted a fixer-upper. I wanted a lot of space, so this was the perfect choice."

Before Isabel had a chance to comment, in traipsed an adorable orange tabby, clearly taking her time with her sizable belly. "Oh my God. That must be Cat."

"Unless I somehow managed to get another one, yes."

Isabel rushed over to her, crouched down and offered her hand. Cat rubbed up against the kitchen island, then did the same to Isabel's fingers. She immediately began to purr, pacing back and forth and brushing Isabel's knees with her tail. "She's so sweet. And so friendly." Isabel went ahead and sat on the floor, Cat purring even more loudly now that Isabel was able to pet her with both hands.

"Yeah. She's been coming to my back door for a while now. I saw her the other morning and it was so cold out, I couldn't leave her out there. My housekeeper put up flyers in the neighborhood and the veterinarian said she isn't microchipped, so we don't know who she belongs to."

"Must just be a neighborhood cat. We had a few of those around when I was growing up. My mom was crazy about cats." Isabel looked up at Jeremy. "They all ended up living at our house in one form or another. Even the ones who were too skittish to come inside got taken to the vet and immunized and fixed. My mom bankrolled it all."

"Wow."

Isabel's heart felt heavy just thinking about her mom. In her mind, she could see her out on their back patio, dishing up wet food for any cat who cared to show up. She talked to them all, gave them all names. She was a woman who was so full of love that showering her kids and husband with it simply wasn't enough. It said a lot about her—Isabel and Sam had never gone a day without feeling truly loved by their mom. "I need to get a kitty when I find a place." She'd never taken the time to get one when she lived in DC, but now that she was shifting her life in a more meaningful direction, a cat or even a few were an obvious choice.

"I know where you can get a pretty cute orange one."

Isabel grinned and looked Cat in the face. "If I

adopt you, you're getting a new and better name. No question about that."

"Go for it."

"Are you seriously not going to keep her?" Isabel asked, getting up from the floor. "She has such a wonderful personality and she seems to be comfortable here."

Cat meowed and rubbed up against Jeremy's leg.

"I'm just not a pet person. My life is so crazy with work, it's hard to imagine caring for another living thing."

Isabel nodded. She'd felt that way for a long time. Not anymore. "Right. Work. I guess you'd better show me to my room so we can get something accomplished today."

Having Isabel in his home—a woman he'd kissed, laughed with, made love to and even argued against—was leaving Jeremy off-balance. A different energy had tiptoed into his private world, and it was both confusing and exhilarating to experience. There was just enough inkling of his past to make him again question what in the world he was doing by allowing himself to be so drawn to her. He and Isabel might be opponents professionally, but there was no denying that they could effortlessly slip into comfortable conversation. They seemed to naturally fall in sync. There was a part of him, deep in his core, that craved that so badly he would do anything to have it. But a bigger part of him had hardened around his needs and desires. That shell was there to protect him, but it was exhausting to carry around all day. He could set it aside when he was at home, and with the snow coming down outside and the weekend stretched out before them, he was in no mood to put it back on again.

With her suitcase in tow, he led her upstairs to the guest room, carrying it inside and setting it down on a bench at the foot of the bed. "It's no Bacharach, but the mattress is incredibly comfortable."

"I'd say it's a big step up for me. I haven't heard a single fire alarm since I got here." Isabel took her handbag and laptop bag and placed them on the bed. She smoothed her hand over the butter-soft duvet. "Ooh. Nice."

Just like the night they met, Jeremy was having to remind himself to slow down. It would be way too easy to kiss her right now and show her exactly how nice that bedding was. "You have your own bath." He traipsed over to the door and flipped on the light for her. When he turned back, she was sitting on the edge of the bed, looking as perfect as he could imagine.

"Thank you. Seriously. This works out great for me, and not just because I needed a place to sleep. I'm eager to get this case squared away. It's of monumental importance."

"To the Eden family or to you?"

"Take your pick. Yes, it's a job, and I'm being paid well to do it, but over the course of the last few weeks, Mindy and her sisters have been amazing to me. They've even invited me to celebrate Christmas with them."

"I thought you didn't celebrate."

"I haven't made the effort, but that doesn't mean I won't take part. I love this time of year and I used to be the sort of person who lived for every minute of Christmas. It's just been a while since I took much joy in it. Like a bad habit, which I suppose is possible for anyone to fall into. Something doesn't feel as good as it used to and so you turn your back on it."

That got the gears in his head going. It was an incredibly insightful thing to say. Jeremy didn't want to tread too heavily on Isabel's personal life, but he was curious. "Any particular reason it stopped feeling good? Work? Career?"

"Work definitely kept me away from it, but this started way before that. My mom. And my dad." She pulled in a breath through her nose, her shoulders rising up to her ears. "They both passed away the same year. It's just been Sam and me since then."

"Oh, wow. I'm so sorry. I didn't know."

She nodded and painted a smile on her face, like she felt a need to comfort him. "So that's why it's important to me to make the Eden sisters happy. You don't luck into a new family very often."

"That sounds nice. A tidy little package." Jeremy decided against giving in to his greatest inclination at the moment, which was to express the depths of his skepticism. In his experience, families like the

Edens would turn their backs on you just as easily as they welcomed you in. "Your brother must be part of this for you, too."

"Absolutely. I love seeing him happy for once in his life, and he's so over the moon for Mindy. They are so in love, it's amazing. I doubt they'll ever get around to planning a real wedding. They just want to get the show on the road."

"I wish them the best of luck."

"Don't you mean happiness?"

"Personally? I think luck plays a much bigger role."

Isabel reached out with her foot and knocked it against his calf. "Hey. That's not nice. They aren't even married yet and you're acting like they're getting ready for a divorce."

Funny, but he never fully appreciated just how pessimistic he'd become until someone took the time to pick apart his words. "You're right. You're absolutely right. Just because I got burned doesn't mean that some people don't have a happy ending."

Isabel reached into her purse and pulled out a lip balm, glossing it over her sumptuous lips. "Sorry. It's so dry out this time of year."

Jeremy cleared his throat, trying to keep from admiring her mouth.

"And it's okay that you're down on love," she continued. "I get it. I've been burned a few times, too."

"Oh yeah? Anybody I know?"

Isabel smirked. "Like I would actually tell you.

And no, I'm guessing you don't know him. He was…" She pursed her lips and furrowed her brow. "Let's just say that he wasn't much for the idea of commitment."

He nodded, knowing all too well what it was like to be on the business end of someone who was willing to take promises and devotion and toss them in the trash. "That's a problem for a lot of guys." It didn't used to be an issue for Jeremy at all. He was once the guy who said "I love you" at the drop of a hat. He used to be the sort of man who made romantic gestures any day of the week, not just on Valentine's Day, Christmas and anniversaries. But when you're endlessly giving, and that generosity is labeled as "not enough," it's hard to see the point in making an effort. At his age, Jeremy wasn't convinced it would ever be worth it to try.

"I was probably asking too much of this guy. But it was just the situation we were in. I try not to harbor too many bad feelings about it. Holding on to that stuff will eat you alive."

"What was he like? The guy who couldn't commit?"

Surprise crossed Isabel's face. "Why do you want to know?"

Jeremy shrugged it off as trivial, but he was so interested in the answer he wasn't sure he could take it if she declined. Perhaps it was because he was still trying so damn hard to figure out what made her tick. "I don't know. Curious, I guess."

She got up from the bed, placed her hand on his shoulder and peered up into his eyes. "Don't worry. He wasn't nearly as cute as you."

Jeremy fought to hold back the full force of the smile that wanted to spread across his face. He loved their back-and-forth. He loved talking to her. For the first time in his entire career, he couldn't have been more excited about negotiations if he tried. "Honestly, I'm surprised you ever had a single man walk away from you. You seem like the type of woman who does the burning."

"I may run hot, but I know better than to set a good thing on fire."

Jeremy swallowed hard.

"And on that note," she said, pulling a legal pad out of her laptop bag, "I think we should get to work."

Nine

The snow kept falling, and Isabel and Jeremy kept working. In the moments when the negotiation grew particularly complicated or even contentious, both Isabel and Jeremy would stare out the window of his home office, watching the fat flakes drift to earth. They were hypnotic and calming, and they both seemed to need the escape, and what a perfect setting, tucked away in Jeremy's cozy office, the room lined with books and decorated with masculine furniture in dark wood and leather.

"It's really coming down out there." Jeremy tossed a pen onto the small conference table they were working at and leaned back in his office chair. He stretched his arms high over his head, causing the hem of his sweater to inch up, revealing a peek of his stomach.

Isabel was nothing if not incredibly distracted by this subtle reminder that her hands, and her mouth for that matter, had once been all over his incredible torso. "It is. The sky's getting dark, too."

Chair tilted back at an angle, Jeremy consulted his watch. "It's nearly five. Do you want to keep going? Or we could take a break."

Isabel flipped through her notes—they'd made so much progress on a compromise for the interest calculations on the loan repayment, along with a schedule for getting Mr. Summers his money. But there were other options she was hoping she'd convince Jeremy to run by his client. "Depends on how generous you're feeling about talking through the alternate forms of repayment I've proposed."

"We've been over this, Isabel. Do you really think that's a good idea? Give my client a chunk of Eden's in exchange for the loan? Right now, both parties despise each other."

"Ten percent is hardly a chunk. It's not like your client would have any control. Just enough to make him a tidy sum every year."

"I really don't see it. With the volatility in retail, I'd have a hard time advising him to take that."

"The store is doing great."

He was still sitting with his chair leaned all the way back, hands clasped and resting on top of his head. He raised both eyebrows and looked down his nose at her. It was inexplicably hot. "If it was truly doing great, you'd be able to fork over the money and we wouldn't be discussing this at all."

"What about a piece of the online business? Would you be happier with that?"

"I'd need to see the numbers."

"Okay, then. Let's get it done."

"Such a shark. Gotta keep swimming, huh?"

"We're so close to figuring this out."

An hour later, everything but the smallest of details had been ironed out. "Did we really just do that?" Jeremy asked, seeming incredulous.

"We did." Isabel surveyed the landscape of the meeting table, which was strewn with papers, files and notes. She couldn't help but feel at least a little jubilant, even though she knew from experience that things could fall apart any time. For now, she would be happy. She held up her hand and reached across the table. "High five?"

"Yes." Jeremy smiled and smacked his hand against hers. "Good job."

From the doorway, Cat meowed loudly, then padded her way to Jeremy. It was at least the fifth or sixth such interruption.

"She seems restless," Isabel said. "I wonder if it's close to kitten time. Has she nested anywhere in the house?"

Jeremy reached down to show Cat some affection. "I have no clue what you're talking about."

"Nesting. Finding herself a safe and cozy spot to have the kittens."

"The vet had me put a blanket in a cardboard box, but I can't get her to stay in it. She's been sleeping on the floor of my closet since she got here."

It was adorable how truly clueless Jeremy was about this. "My guess is she's planning on giving birth in there."

"Seriously?" His eyes went wide with horror. "In my closet?"

"Why don't you show me?"

"Yeah. Absolutely. No more reason to hang out in here today."

Jeremy got up from his chair and Isabel followed him out of the room, down the hall to the last door on the left. Inside was a magnificent and sumptuous bedroom, tastefully decorated with a warm touch. The bed seemed to go on forever, with a charcoal-gray duvet and plump pillows. Overhead, a wrought iron chandelier gave the space a soft glow. The windows, overlooking the back patio, brought in the perfect amount of natural light.

"No wonder you've never needed a sleep mask. This room is so peaceful. I think I could sleep in here for days."

Jeremy smiled. "You don't need that thing at home, do you? I mean, if you aren't staying in a hotel?"

Isabel brushed her fingers on the silky soft bedding. "Depends on how worn out I am." She instantly regretted her choice of words, especially when Jeremy cocked an eyebrow.

Cat sauntered into the room and darted right into the closet.

"I'm telling you, you're about to have a bunch of kittens in with your designer suits and Italian leather shoes." Isabel nodded at the closet. "May I?"

"Please. Be my guest."

Isabel stepped inside and Jeremy was right behind her, flipping on the light. Either Jeremy was an incredibly smart man or his ex had been highly concerned with her appearance. His closet had the sort of lighting you find at a cosmetics counter, gentle enough to make anyone look amazing. Which of course meant that Jeremy appeared flawless, even with his stubble showing the effects of late day.

"She's been sleeping down here." Jeremy pulled back a row of dress shirts to reveal the back corner, where sure enough, Cat had made herself a bed. "Hey. Wait a minute. That's my favorite T-shirt." He crouched down. Isabel knelt next to him. "I wondered where that went. I took it off the other morning to take a shower after my workout and never saw it again."

Isabel was momentarily stuck on the mental image of Jeremy in the shower, with droplets of water on his chest. She'd never wanted so badly to have a bar of soap in her hands. "Did you think it just disappeared? She clearly stole it. Dragged it in here to make her bed."

He shook his head in disbelief. "I figured I must have tossed it in the hamper and didn't remember doing it. I have a lot on my mind these days."

She couldn't help but notice the weighty drag in his voice. Not putting much thought into it, she placed her hand on the center of his back to comfort him, but that caused him to look at her, his gray eyes showing mysterious flecks of blue in this light. If they were a window into his soul, she wished she could see some true happiness in there. She was desperate for a reason *not* to kiss him. Make him happy. She could do that, at least for a little while, with the snow falling heavily outside.

Jeremy cleared his throat and returned his sights to Cat's nest. "I can't believe she stole my stinky, sweaty T-shirt."

"It means she loves you. Pets love things that smell like their owners."

"I'm not her owner. This is temporary." He stood up and stepped away, as if that could somehow extricate him from the situation.

"Uh-huh. Tell that to Cat."

He turned back to her, kneading his forehead. "How do I get her to not have the kittens in here? Won't it make a big mess?"

"First off, you don't get her to do anything. If she's happy and feels safe there, you should let her do her thing. You do not want to get into a battle of wills with a mama cat. Second, we can put down an old towel or two and you can toss them out once the kittens arrive."

"What about the T-shirt?"

She patted his shoulder in consolation. "I think that's pretty much a goner."

"I never should have let her in that morning."

"Oh, Jeremy, no. You had to do it. She could have died out there. Her and her kittens. You did the right thing."

He twisted his lips, which made her think he was considering the other side of the coin she'd just shown him. "You really are good at forming an argument."

She loved not only knowing that she could show him when he was wrong, but that he would actually listen. She found that a rare quality in a man, especially a lawyer. "Thanks. I appreciate that. Now what do I have to do to convince you to open a bottle of wine?"

"You don't. It's six on a Friday and there's cause for celebration. I can't believe it's taken us this long to get around to it."

"You're speaking my language. I'm just going to grab my purse from the guest room. I can't live this time of year without lip balm."

Down the hall they went, making a brief stop so Isabel could fetch her bag, then descending the stairs and back to the kitchen. Isabel perched on a barstool at the kitchen island and watched Jeremy go to work. "Red or white?" he asked.

She glanced out the patio windows. The snow was still pretty and fluffy, but the wind had started to whip. "Considering the weather? Definitely red."

"Perfect. I have a Spanish rioja that's absolutely delicious."

"Sounds amazing."

Jeremy opened a tall cabinet at the far end of the kitchen, which had a waist-high wine chiller below and diagonal bottle storage above, the entire setup going from floor to ceiling.

"It's like your own little cellar."

"There's a real cellar downstairs on the ground floor. I got really into wine about ten years ago. I was starting to wonder if I was going to be a bachelor forever, so I figured I might get a hobby." He brought the bottle to the island and expertly opened it, then pulled two glasses from an upper cabinet near the fridge.

"And then you met the woman you married and the bachelor was reformed?" Isabel was indeed curious about the notion of Jeremy seeing himself as never getting married, and that apparently changing at some point.

"It had nothing to do with being reformed. I was on board from the beginning."

"Head over heels?"

"I guess you could say that, but she also had a way of sweeping you up into her world. Or maybe sucking you into the eye of her personal hurricane is a more apt analogy."

"She sounds lovely."

Jeremy laughed. "It happened fast. That's all I can tell you. I think she liked the fact that I wasn't the typical Manhattan playboy. She'd dated a lot of guys like that." He filled their glasses and handed her one. "Cheers. To not talking about my ex-wife."

Isabel took a quick sip. "It's delicious. Thank you. But not so fast." She had questions. A lot of questions. Things weren't entirely adding up. "Okay, confession time. I looked you up on the internet after the first meeting at your office."

"Of course you did."

"You did the same thing to me, did you not?"

He brought his glass around to the other side of the island, but didn't sit with her. "Come on. If we're going to talk about this, we're going in the living room. I'd rather be comfortable while discussing unpleasant subjects." He didn't wait for her reply, but instead wandered off.

Isabel followed in earnest, worried she'd hurt him. "I don't mean for it to be unpleasant. I'm just curious because what you're telling me isn't matching up with what I read."

He set his glass and the bottle on the coffee table and began building a fire in the fireplace, crumpling up newspaper, then stacking logs across it and striking a match. She stood and watched him work. "Isabel. As a former Washington, DC, lawyer with a bunch of very high-profile clients, I have to think that you would know better than anyone that what's in the paper isn't always the full story. A lot of it has to do with who gets there first."

"Well, sure. Things get twisted. But they don't usually take a one-eighty."

He stood and brushed his hands off on his pants, then pointed to the couch. "Please. Sit."

She felt like she was in trouble, and just like upstairs when he'd admonished her during negotiations, she found it incredibly sexy. "Yes, sir." She did as she was told, sinking down into the comfortable cushions. The fire began to crackle and blaze. Between the wine and Jeremy, she never wanted to leave the room.

"Actually, a one-eighty is the perfect way to spin something." He took a long draw of his wine and Isabel admired his profile in the golden glow of the fire. "It's a believable story since it's true, so you simply take whatever you're guilty of and accuse the other person of it."

"So if I'm a woman who wants out of my marriage, but I'm worried about how that will be perceived, I tell the press that my husband isn't the settling-down type, or that he isn't loving."

He turned to her, his eyes full of resignation. She'd seen this expression from him before, the look of someone who was hurt and sad, but who had learned to live with it. Isabel hated the idea that anyone would have to live that way, especially a man as extraordinary as Jeremy. "Precisely."

Isabel took another sip of her wine, her mind still

churning. No wonder the things she'd read about Jeremy had seemed so off. "I almost hate to ask this..."

A corner of his mouth shot up in a wry smile. "You don't hate to ask anything."

She leaned forward and grasped his forearm. "No. I really don't want to upset you. Truly. I don't. You've been nothing but gracious in letting me stay here."

"Go for it. I have no secrets."

Isabel found herself hoping that was really true. Because every minute with Jeremy was starting to feel like the start of something.

I really don't want to upset you. Even though Isabel was capable of a good sneak attack, he was sure of what she was about to ask. He'd never spoken about it to anyone. His parents spent their time making themselves the victims by claiming their own embarrassment at the way their son had been dragged through the tabloids. His friends made themselves scarce after the divorce. Nobody wanted to go out to dinner with the guy who was getting snide comments from perfect strangers who'd sided with the socialite. So Jeremy kept it all bottled up inside, another attempt at holding on to his pride.

"I shouldn't ask," she said. "Let's talk about something else."

"No. Please. Just do it. Let's put the whole thing to rest. Honestly, it'll be a relief."

"Was it all a one-eighty? There was a suggestion that you'd been unfaithful." She held up a finger.

"And before you answer, I want to make it clear that I will not judge you. Everyone has their reasons for doing things."

Jeremy had every reason in the world to keep a wall up with Isabel, both personal and professional. But the reality of their situation was that they were close to wrapping up negotiations. Their clients would come away happy. As for the personal side, she was so easy to talk to. It had been like that from the moment he'd met her. There was something almost therapeutic about baring his soul to her. "Everything she did to sabotage our marriage, or every unpleasant feeling she had, she put on me. The thing about not being made for commitment, the thing about not being the settling-down type. So yes, there was infidelity, and it was all hers."

"I'm so sorry. That's such a terrible betrayal."

She wasn't wrong. It had been. But now that it was years later and he couldn't imagine himself with Kelsey at all, the pain wasn't quite so persistent. "I didn't find out about the affair until after she left. I've somehow convinced myself that it wasn't that bad because I didn't know about it while it was going on. That might be some faulty logic at work."

"Those are the things we say when we're trying to protect ourselves. There's only so much hurt a person can endure."

"Is there really a maximum? Sometimes life keeps throwing stuff at you, whether you want it or not."

"I have to ask why you didn't stand up to her. You

had no comment in the article I read. I have a hard time imagining you taking that lying down. A lawyer always fights back."

"But a lawyer also knows when to quit. Some battles just aren't worth it. Plus, who wants to get into a fight over love? In the newspapers? Either it's there between you or it isn't. You can't just pull it out of thin air. And it wasn't like I was going to convince her to come back."

He watched as she sank farther back against the cushions, wineglass in hand. What kind of pain had she endured? Was that why she sometimes seemed like such a mystery? "Now that I told you my sad story, I want to know if I can ask about the guy who burned you."

She looked down into the rioja in her glass, swirling it round and round. "Bad timing. It wasn't all his fault. It was an unfortunate situation."

"Those are an awful lot of vague details."

"Okay, then. Here are the specifics. I got pregnant and he panicked. He couldn't handle it. We'd only been going out about six months and it had been very casual." She breathed deeply and sighed. "So I did him a favor and I called if off. I already knew that I wanted to have a baby, so I decided I would just deal with it on my own, but then life decided to throw me the cruelest of curveballs when I lost the pregnancy." Her voice cracked when she uttered those last few words. The room fell impossibly quiet.

"I'm so sorry. That must have been awful."

"Nobody knows about it. I mean, he must have figured it out when I never had a baby, but it's not like he ever checked in on me or asked."

"You never told your brother what happened?"

A sad smile crossed her lips. "You know, I thought about it, but I don't think Sam would have dealt very well with it. I think it would have made him feel helpless, and I didn't see any good in that. So I dusted myself off and I went back to work and I tried to forget."

She was so tough. So resilient. No wonder she made such an excellent attorney. "Back to being a shark?"

"That's the last thing I am." Isabel waved it off.

"A beautiful shark, of course."

Her eyes flashed in the soft light from the fireplace. "Flattery will get you everywhere."

"I'm no dummy."

"And I'm serious when I say I'm not a shark. It's an act. Acting is how you win. You can't tell me you aren't the same way."

"I'm not acting right now."

Cocking her head to one side, a dark strand of her hair fell across her cheek. The way she narrowed her sights on him made him feel as vulnerable as he'd felt in a very long time. "I believe that. But when you're working, you have on your armor. You're ready for battle. And if I'm being completely honest, I think you were playing an act the night we met."

Jeremy reached for the wine bottle and poured

more into her glass before topping off his own. "Isn't everyone on their best behavior when they first meet? Trying to impress the other person?"

"Yes, and that's why I didn't want to talk about work. I wanted us to just be a man and a woman having a conversation."

"And you think I was faking my way through it? I guarantee you, I didn't fake a damn thing up in your room. That was all legit."

Isabel grinned, her cheeks flushing pink. "I believe that. I do. It's the first part of the night when you were acting. Playing the part of the fun-loving guy."

"Hey. I love fun. I just don't have a lot of it."

"But you're not as cavalier as you try to make yourself seem. You act like nothing bothers you, but you aren't like that. You're thoughtful and serious." She took another sip of her wine, then scooted closer on the couch. "And now that you've told me the story about your marriage, I know why. You're trying to hide your pain from everyone."

Jeremy swallowed back the emotion of having her see right through him. "I just don't want to feel hurt anymore. That's all that is. So I pretend like it's not there and I figure it'll eventually go away."

Slowly and evenly, she nodded, gazing up at him with her sweet and tenderhearted eyes. He loved that she had so many sides, that she was a woman of many facets. She could be determined one minute and gentle the next. "I know. I just want you to know that you don't have to pretend with me." She ran her finger around the rim of her wineglass. "We're nearly off the clock."

"Just a man and a woman having a conversation."

"No hiding."

Two simple words from Isabel and a wave of heat rose in Jeremy, starting in his thighs and rolling upward, taking hold in his hips, stomach and chest. He fixed his gaze on her, on the rise and fall of her breaths, the flush in her cheeks, the brilliant flash of life in her eyes. Electricity was arcing between them. A current. A jolt. One minute they were talking work and life and pain and now...well, he would have had to be a complete idiot to not notice that this was all leading somewhere he hadn't quite planned on.

What was it about Isabel that didn't merely tug at his heartstrings, but unraveled them? It was more than attraction, although that was its own powerful force. There was a connection between them, one that went beyond working together.

"I was hiding from you this week." The words rolled out of his mouth as if he'd planned to say them all along, which he hadn't at all, but it still felt good to own up to it. So good that he wanted to keep going. "That night at dinner, all I wanted to do was kiss you. But the pressure is on with this case and I worried I would end up sabotaging myself if I spent any time with you."

"So you invited me here because you didn't have a choice."

He shook his head. "No. I invited you because I had a reason. I finally had a legitimate reason to do what I'd wanted to do all along."

"I have an admission of my own." She sat forward, angling her body toward his.

Jeremy's pulse picked up, running along at a clip. "I'm listening."

"I thought about kissing you way before dinner. I thought about it that day in your office."

All he wanted was for her to bend at the waist and plant her soft lips on his. He wanted to feel her body pressed against his. He wanted to get lost in her and never be found. "And since then?"

"There's been a lot of inner conflict over it." She licked her lower lip and placed her wineglass on the coffee table, which felt like an ultimatum—kiss me, or don't.

Jeremy didn't want to leave any challenge from Isabel unaccepted.

Ten

Isabel was tired of waiting. She had to have Jeremy. The trouble was, the fragile parts of her ego really wanted him to make the first move. And he was being the perfect gentleman. Apparently setting aside her wineglass and biting down on her lower lip were not enough of an invitation.

She scooted closer to him on the couch, pulling her leg up all the way onto the cushion and facing him. Looking at him was both the easiest thing in the world and the most difficult—he was so handsome, it made the center of her chest burn. The fire popped and crackled, the heat warming one side of her face. He tossed back the last of his wine, as if needing liquid encouragement, and there was a very big part of her that wanted to just come out and say it—*I want you, Jeremy. Now.*

He finally placed his own glass on the table and turned to her, his eyes beautifully dark with desire. She'd wanted plenty of men in her lifetime, but none as bad as Jeremy. None so bad that it made it hard to breathe. Whether it was unfinished business or the notion of false starts, they both deserved this.

"I don't want you to feel as though I'm taking advantage," he said, reaching for her hand, caressing her fingers softly. "It's my house and you're vulnerable here."

Isabel's heart *and* body were aching for his touch. "I don't know that I've ever felt more comfortable. Anywhere." She inched herself closer until their knees were touching, then she took his other hand and raised it to her lips. Even that one touch of skin against skin left her nearly gasping for more. She had to be closer. She had to be next to him. And it had to happen now.

Isabel shifted up onto her knees and straddled Jeremy's lap. The pleased look on his face was her reward for bravery. She let her weight settle, pressing her hips into his, already the heat and need pooling between her legs. Her hands went to the hem of her sweater and she pulled it up over her head, her hair collapsing around her shoulders when she cast the garment aside. She loved falling under his appraisal, his dark eyes scanning her body. She didn't need him to tell her she was beautiful. She saw it all in his expression.

The first kiss was the softest, as if they were marking the moment. The beginning. His lips were just as firm and perfect as she remembered. Possibly more so. She set her elbows on his shoulders and dug her fingers into his thick hair, rocking her center against his. She could already feel how hard he was, even through the layers of denim between them. Their tongues wound together. He ran his across her lower lip. His warm hands roved the landscape of her back, then he finally had the good sense to remove her shirt and unhook her bra, pulling the straps forward to be rid of it. He took her breasts in his hands, cupping them completely and rolling her nipples between his fingers. Her skin gathered and grew hard beneath his touch, the perfect contrast to the softness of the kiss. But she wanted his lips and tongue everywhere, so she wrenched her mouth from his.

He took the invitation, licking and sucking one nipple, then the other, his hands squeezing her breasts firmly. Electricity zapped from her chest straight to her center, as if there were a line connecting the two. It felt so good that she wanted to close her eyes and simply languish in the sensation, but it was so hot to watch his face as he flicked his tongue against the tight buds of sensitive skin. Isabel curled her fingers into his shoulders, letting her nails dig into his skin. Jeremy's eyes popped open and he looked up at her, their gazes connecting before he took a gentle bite of her nipple. It was the perfect amount of pain, just enough to show how much he wanted her. It took every bit of pent-up desire inside her and ratcheted it up another notch.

Isabel reached down and lifted his sweater up over his head, spreading her hands across his glorious chest, firm and muscled with the perfect amount of hair. She kissed one sculpted shoulder, then across his clavicle, nestling her face in his neck, letting the stubble scratch at her nose and cheek while she inhaled his warm smell. Jeremy's hands were at both of her hips, squeezing hard and pulling her against him even more tightly. White-hot liquid heat pooled between her legs as she felt his erection against her center.

Both of his hands traveled north to the middle of her back and the next thing she knew, he had shifted her until she was lying back on the couch, the leather cool against her overheated skin. Jeremy stood and shucked his jeans and boxers, never taking his eyes off her. He was everything she wanted, long and lean and so primed for her that it was impossible to not feel lucky. She wedged her mind in the moment and focused on the physical, like the way her need picked up when she watched him take his steely length into his own hand and give it a few careful strokes. She loved seeing his own hand on his body, but it also made her desperate to touch him.

Isabel unbuttoned her jeans and lifted her hips off the couch, shimmying them and her panties down her legs. Jeremy helped her pull them from her ankles

and then she was completely bare to him, ready and
dying to have him inside her. "Come here," she said,
her voice sounding a bit desperate.

"I want to see you touch yourself," he replied.

Isabel wasn't much of an exhibitionist, but Jeremy had her so turned on right now, she would have
done anything he wanted. She dropped one foot to the
floor and eased her knee up, spreading her legs. She
brushed her fingertips against her chest, down along
the flat plane of skin between her breasts. The anticipation on Jeremy's face was priceless. He watched
her, both enthralled and speechless, standing next to
her and stroking his erection. She studied what he
liked, even as she relished her own touch as her fingers rode down her belly and finally between her legs.

A gasp left her lips when she touched her apex,
the skin warm and slick with desire. She began to
move her fingers in delicate circles, feeling as though
she could rocket into space in no time at all if she
wasn't careful. Jeremy lowered himself to a kneeling
position before her, kissing the knee of the leg that
was still up on the couch. Isabel didn't stop with the
ministrations, even when it was pushing her even
closer to her peak. She wanted to see what he would
do next. She was desperate for it.

He kissed his way along her inner thigh and she
moved her hands out of the way to comb his thick
hair as he moved lower. His mouth found her center
and he used his fingers to gently spread her folds and
give himself better access. As hot as it was, Isabel's

eyes clamped shut as he drove her to her peak with his tongue, which traveled in circles hard against her. She did her best to hold off on the pressure, but it eventually became too much, and she felt the dam break, the way her body gave in to him completely. She knocked her head back and called out as she rode out wave after wave of warmth and pleasure. On the other side of the room, the fire continued to roar, but Isabel knew that the heat coming from it was only a fraction of what Jeremy was about to give to her.

Jeremy took one more taste of Isabel, wanting to be immersed in the sensory delights of her unbelievably gorgeous body. Everything about her was soft and sweet, yet hot and carnal. If things between them never went any further than tonight, at least he'd always have the mental image of her touching herself, of her fingers rolling over her most delicate places, while the heat of the room flushed her skin with a breathtaking shade of pink.

But right now, he had more pressing needs. He had to be inside her. Isabel pulled her legs back, then knelt down next to him on the floor and pushed the coffee table a good foot or so away from them. Jeremy stretched out on the plush area rug as Isabel positioned herself between his knees, taking his throbbing erection into her hands and stroking delicately. Everything in his body went tight—his abs, his hips and thighs. She took her time and he loved watching as her slender fingers rode his length, up and down. As good as it felt, he wanted more of her, and as if she knew what he was thinking, she lowered her head and took him between her plump lips.

Her tongue was hot and wet on his skin, which was already straining from the tension. He couldn't think of another time he'd been so hard or wanted a woman so badly. He gently rolled his fingers through her silky hair as she swirled her tongue and made it nearly impossible to think about anything other than pleasure and warmth. Just when he was starting to feel as though he couldn't take much more of the pressure, Isabel released him from her mouth, kissing his lower belly.

"Don't move. I'm going to get a condom from my purse." She flitted off to the kitchen and was back in seconds, tearing open the packet and kneeling next to him. She then climbed on top of him, taking his length in her hand and guiding him inside.

As she sank down on top of him, he marveled at how well they fit together, how this was even better than that first night together, when logic said that it could never be better because the excitement of everything new tends to eclipse the familiar. They moved together, perfectly in sync, and Isabel lowered her head to kiss him. Their tongues wound together as his fingers roamed down her back to the velvety skin of her bottom, his hands encouraging her to raise her hips as far as she could, only because it felt so damn good to have her ride his entire length.

The pressure was building in his hips, and everything was pulling tight again. Isabel's breaths were ragged, but he wanted her closer before he came, so he slipped one of his hands between their bodies and found her center with his thumb. She countered with pressure of her own, pressing her pelvis into his harder and harder, grinding her body in a circle with every pass.

Isabel rounded her back, using her hips to force him closer to his peak. He clamped his eyes shut and his body gave way, pleasure pulsing and slamming into him. Isabel followed mere seconds later, burying her face in his neck and rotating her hips, making the final waves longer and even more pleasurable. She collapsed on top of him, warm and a bit sweaty, resting her head against his chest. He wrapped his arms around her tightly and kissed the top of her head over and over again. There were no words between them and Jeremy felt that was only fitting. They had exchanged plenty of them in the few short weeks they'd known each other. It was nice to get back to a place where they could let actions speak louder than words.

She rolled to his side and curled into him. He wrapped his arm around her waist and for a moment, they both got lost in the warm flicker of the fire. This was not how he'd imagined tonight going, but if he was being honest, it was everything he ever could have hoped for.

Eleven

Jeremy woke with a feeling he hadn't had in a long time—hope. He was also drunk on infatuation. Isabel was simply amazing, and last night had been unbelievable. Everything he'd thought about their sexual chemistry had been on the money. He hadn't made it up.

"Good morning, beautiful," he said, kissing her bare shoulder.

She smiled, eyes still closed, lying on her stomach. The early light of day filtered in through the windows, bathing her in a bright and beautiful glow. "Good morning."

He cozied up next to her, their naked bodies pressed together. It was so good to not wake up alone. "What do you want to do today?"

In response, Isabel's stomach rumbled loudly. "Food might be a good idea."

"We never ate last night, did we?"

She opened an eye and popped up onto her elbow. "We did not. I feel like I should file a complaint, except you're still way ahead of the Bacharach. Not a single siren went off in the middle of the night."

"We never would've met if it weren't for that silly alarm."

She rolled to her back and clutched the covers to her chest. "We still would have met. It just would've been under far different circumstances."

Their first rendezvous had set the stage for last night, so he was immensely thankful that things had played out the way they had. "I'm glad the first time we encountered each other wasn't at the negotiating table."

"Me, too." She leaned forward and kissed him. "Now let's get some food. I'm starving."

Downstairs in the kitchen, Jeremy put some bacon in a skillet and began cracking eggs for breakfast. Cat had come downstairs for her own morning meal, which Isabel dished up for her before taking a seat at the center island. "I like watching a man cook."

"Lots of years as a bachelor," he said. "And my ex didn't cook anyway, so it was all up to me." Looking back, he should have known it was never going to last. Kelsey spent too little time in this house. She was always, desperate for her next adventure. It had taken a long time for him to figure out that her absence wasn't about him. It was about the bottomless hole in her psyche that would always need filling.

"What did you and your wife plan to do with all of this space anyway?"

Jeremy dished up the bacon and eggs and grabbed slices of buttered toast, then ferried the plates to the island. "Madam, your breakfast is served."

Her entire face lit up when she smiled. "Thank you, sir."

He took the seat next to her. "I assumed we would have kids, and if we were going to create our dream house, it only seemed logical to me that we would have space for a growing family. That never happened, obviously. I wanted kids and she did not."

Isabel sipped her coffee, hands wrapped around the mug. "Did you guys not talk about it ahead of time? That's a pretty important topic before marriage."

"We did discuss it. I told her that I wanted a family and she said she did, too. But when it came time to try to get pregnant, she kept secretly taking her birth control pills. I guess she just never had the guts to tell me she'd changed her mind. Or she'd been lying to me all along." He was proud of himself for saying all of that without losing his cool. Something about Isabel made it so easy to confide in her. "Maybe I'm not cut out for parenthood, anyway. My own parents did not embrace their role."

"I wouldn't call your dad warm and fuzzy. At least what I saw of him."

Jeremy had to laugh, even if it was a sound born of sadness. "He's not. Neither is my mom, unfortunately. Although she has a softer edge to her. I'll give her that much. They've both always been more interested in what a person accomplishes than what kind of person they are."

"That's terrible."

"They've always been like that and I fed into it. I learned from an early age that if I did exactly what they wanted, and especially if I excelled at it, I was showered with praise. That was as close as they came to expressing affection."

"Is that why you became a lawyer?"

"Actually, it isn't. My dad wanted me to follow in his footsteps, but it was my grandfather who inspired me to do it. He was all about the subtleties of the law and he loved the interpretation of it. He loved forming an argument." Jeremy turned to Isabel. "Very much like you, actually."

"He sounds like an awesome guy."

"He was. Those are all his law books in my office upstairs."

"So that's why you like to work here. Stay away from your dad and be surrounded by reminders of the real reason you got into this crazy business in the first place."

"Absolutely." Jeremy nodded, perhaps a little too eagerly. Isabel was an angel who'd dropped out of the sky. She understood him so naturally. "So, I was thinking, since it's Saturday and there are only a few days until Christmas, maybe we could do something holiday-related today."

"What did you have in mind? I hope not caroling. I'm a terrible singer."

"You and me both." He took another bite of his toast. "Shopping? I've already done mine. I get the same thing for my parents every year." A year's supply of monogrammed golf balls for his dad, who not only hit the links regularly, he was apt to lose them in the water hazards. For his mom, Jeremy went to Tiffany & Co. and bought the most recent offerings of earrings or a bracelet.

"I'm done, too. I got everything at Eden's. It was the first time in years that I've done that." She slid him a glance. "What about decorating? A Christmas tree?"

"I don't have an artificial one. There's a tree lot about seven or eight blocks away. Even with the snow, it's probably open. We could drag it back?"

Isabel turned and looked out the patio doors. "We don't need to buy one. You already have plenty."

"Out there?" This option had never occurred to him. Not once.

"Do you have any lights? Ornaments?"

"Well, yeah. I haven't used them since my divorce, but they're definitely still there."

"Let's decorate one of the trees out on your patio.

It'll be so pretty at night. Plus you won't have to worry about Cat climbing it or messing around with it."

"You want to go out there in the cold? And decorate one of the cypress trees?"

"It's not snowing anymore. The sun is shining. It'll be nice. Plus, it'll be good to get some fresh air."

This was about the craziest idea Jeremy had ever heard. And he loved it. "We'll go hunting for everything in the attic in a little bit."

"We have all day, don't we?"

After breakfast was done and the kitchen cleaned, they trekked upstairs to the top floor of the house, where the attic was. It wasn't difficult to find the boxes of Christmas decor. They were some of the only things up there—thus was the life of the single guy with too much space. Jeremy certainly hesitated before he opened the first box. He and Kelsey had bought these decorations together, back when he believed they were building a life and would use them for years to come. Back when he'd thought that they might have kids and those children would eventually hang these ornaments on the tree. He didn't want to think about it too much as a reflection of the life he no longer had. Here with Isabel, his heart was nothing but light. If she'd never come along, these Christmas baubles might have spent many more years tucked away in an attic, collecting dust and going unused and unappreciated. It wasn't difficult to see the parallel between the boxes of ornaments and his own existence.

"I think four strands of lights will be enough. And I think these red and silver ball ornaments will stand up to the elements." Isabel tapped a fingernail against the shiny orbs. "They don't seem particularly breakable."

"Perfect."

They carried the boxes down a floor, then each went and changed into more suitable clothes for outdoors—jeans and sweaters. Back downstairs, they bundled up in boots, coats and gloves. "Do you have an extra hat I can wear?" she asked. "I don't have one with me and it looks really cold out there."

"I'm sure I have something."

Jeremy rummaged through his front coat closet, where he pulled out a red hat he'd had for years. "I haven't worn this one since college." He tugged it on her head, which pulled much of her hair over her face. With his fingers, he gently brushed it aside, tucking it neatly under the cap. She looked up at him while he did it, eyes big and bright, leaving him with only one logical thing to say. "You're so beautiful, Isabel. Truly." He was so deep in her orbit right now, it would be difficult to ever pull himself out. He wasn't sure he'd ever want to.

"You aren't half bad yourself, you know." Leaning into him, she slowly rose up onto her tiptoes and placed a soft kiss on his lips.

All he wanted to do was melt into her. Stay like this forever. *You're perfect. You're the best thing that's happened to me in recent history.* The words were right there, zipping around in his head, desperately wanting to be set free. But Jeremy knew his worst tendencies, the way he wanted to jump many steps ahead and profess his affection. It didn't matter how amazing she was. It was too soon. "Ready for our Christmas tree adventure?"

"I was born ready."

Isabel was beginning to think she'd gravely misjudged Jeremy that first night they met. Normally, she was an exceptional judge of character from the get-go. She was good at picking up on signals—the little things people do that tell you what drives them or makes them tick. The talent was part and parcel of being a lawyer and it'd been honed over the years. If anything, she should be getting better at it, not worse.

So where did she go wrong with Jeremy? Or was it simply that he was putting on an act, the one that kept him from sharing his pain with the rest of the world? She couldn't decide which it was, but also decided that it didn't truly matter. For the first time in years, she was actually enjoying herself. And she wasn't about to let her overthinking ways come between herself and a good time.

Trudging out onto the snow-covered patio with Jeremy, Isabel realized this suggestion of hers had been a bit unorthodox. "Thanks for indulging my peculiar idea."

"Are you kidding?" Jeremy asked, swiping snow from a patio table to give them a spot to put the boxes. "This is far less work than dragging a Christmas tree seven or eight blocks."

"It's more eco-friendly if you think about it, too. This tree's already here."

Jeremy trekked over to the back door and plugged in an extension cord, then returned to Isabel so they could begin stringing the lights. They worked in tandem, with her uncoiling the strands around her arm and Jeremy climbing up on a patio chair to loop them around the tree. It was a bright and sunny day, the air perfectly crisp and cold. Despite the temperature, Jeremy had opted for no hat, which gave her the perfect view of his adorable forehead wrinkles as he concentrated so intently on the task before him.

"I know it's probably my job to tell you where you missed a spot, but you're doing an amazing job," she said. "Not surprising. You're pretty much perfect at everything you do."

Jeremy looked down at her so abruptly that his sunglasses slid to the end of his nose. "You have got to be kidding."

"Um. No. I'm not."

Shaking his head in disbelief, he placed the remainder of the final strand of lights. "We'll have to wait until it's dark to see how it turned out." He then climbed down from the chair and opened one of the ornament boxes.

"I was serious about what I said. You're an amazing lawyer. Negotiating with you was one of the highlights of my entire career."

That stopped him dead in his tracks. "You're the one who's amazing." He swiped off his sunglasses and before Isabel really knew what was happening, he had his arms around her. His mouth was on hers, passionate and giving. It sent ripples of excitement through her entire body. She couldn't wait to go back inside with him.

"Wow," she muttered, sounding and feeling drunk.

"You make me want to do things like that, Isabel. You make me feel good. In every way imaginable."

Funny how making someone else happy could be such a lift to your own spirits. Not that Isabel needed a lift—she was already floating on air. "You make me feel good, too."

They finished the tree and headed back inside, stomping the snow from their boots and peeling off the winter layers. The moment clothes of any sort started to come off, it all had to go. Jeremy approached Isabel like a man on the hunt, lifting her sweater up over her head, peeling her bra strap from her shoulder and kissing her bare skin.

She shuddered, in part from his touch and in part from the ambient temperature in the room. "There's too much cold air from outside down here. Let's go upstairs to your bedroom."

He took her hand and led her through the house, zeroing in on his bed, sitting on the edge of the mattress and encouraging her to stand between his knees. He kissed her stomach, kneaded her breasts, and then pulled her down on top of him. She felt like a goddess, so admired and adored. That alone was nearly enough to send her into oblivion. The rest of their clothes were gone in a flash and they became a frantic tangle of limbs, mouths roaming and craving caresses. Isabel gasped when Jeremy drove inside her, relishing every delicious inch of him. He took deep strokes and kissed her neck, scratching at her tender skin with the stubble on his face. She wrapped her legs around his waist and used her feet to hold him tighter. It didn't take long until he left her unraveling, calling his name and breathless.

Jeremy climbed out of bed and pulled back the covers, Isabel quickly ducking under them to get warm. With the postorgasmic glow taking over, and after their eventful morning, she craved sleep. Her eyelids were heavy, her mind fuzzy. "You wore me out, Sharp. I guess all of that fresh air and sex did me in."

"Take a nap. You work like crazy and this weekend should be for relaxing. Plus, I remember that you told me the night we met that it's one of your favorite things."

Isabel grinned at the memory of them sharing their three universal truths that night. "It's the truth. I absolutely love it."

Jeremy reached over onto his nightstand for a book. "Perfect. You nap. I'll read."

When Isabel woke, she was nothing if not disoriented. Jeremy was gone, the room dark. She squinted at his clock: 5:12 p.m. She'd taken a three-hour nap, so much longer than she would normally sleep during the day. As she slowly woke, delicious smells filtered to her nose—garlic, herbs and possibly wine. Jeremy must have started dinner.

She padded down the hall to the guest room to grab a cardigan, popping into her bathroom to freshen her makeup while she was at it. Still not quite awake, she knocked one of her toiletry bags from the counter, sending the contents flying. She crouched down to pick up the mess, but her hand froze on a small box of tampons. For a moment, she stared at the blue-and-yellow swirl pattern on the package. It was as if she was standing on the edge of a realization, and reality was about to push her over the edge. *I'm late.*

Frantically, she fished her phone out of her pocket and pulled up the app she used to track her cycle. She was remarkably calm despite what the notification on her screen was telling her—she was six days late. Maybe this was the upside of having been a high-powered attorney for so long. Most panic-laden situations did not make Isabel freak out. Even when she could potentially have a very big reason for going into a tizzy.

Could she have gotten pregnant the night of the broken condom? It was the only possible explanation. Jeremy was the only man she'd been with in the last year. And if that was the case, what was she supposed to do about it? What would it mean? They were getting along amazingly and had an unbelievable chemistry, but this was going to throw everything on a fast track that Jeremy couldn't possibly be prepared for. If he'd gone into a panic over the broken condom, she couldn't imagine him reacting well to news of an actual baby.

She sucked in a deep breath. She had to get her act together. Phone still in hand, she flicked over to a different app and placed an order from the chain drugstore nearby. They could deliver her a pregnancy test tomorrow, along with a few other things to help hide the contents of the order, and she could take it Monday morning if she hadn't started her period by then. It was the responsible thing to do, most likely completely unnecessary. She typed in Jeremy's address, clicked Place Order and shoved her phone back into her pocket. It was probably nothing. Just her cycle being wonky.

When she reached the main floor and rounded the staircase to walk to the back of the house, she saw the tree lit up out on the patio. She ambled along the main corridor, her pulse thumping in her chest, while the aromas from the kitchen enticed her to move a little more quickly. She *was* hungry. And she'd been incredibly tired.

"Hey there, sleepyhead," Jeremy said, turning away from the stove.

Isabel's heart did a full cartwheel at the sight of him. "Are you making me dinner?"

"I'm making up for last night and the noticeable

lack of food." He wrapped his arm around her shoulders and gave her a soft kiss.

"It smells amazing. Although I hope that doesn't mean we don't get to revisit the events of last night. Or this morning. Or this afternoon."

Jeremy slipped his hand under her jaw and brought her lips to his. The kiss was enough to make her lose all sense of time and place, which was perfect. She couldn't stack another worry inside her head. "I can't wait to do everything we did last night."

"Neither can I." Goose bumps raced over the surface of her skin and she focused on the thrill of being with him.

"Did you see the tree?" He took her hand and led her to the patio doors. "It's so beautiful. You're a genius. I'm going to do this every year from now on."

"How wonderful. A new tradition." Isabel leaned into him and put her arm around his waist. The lights twinkled in the inky darkness outside and the wind blew enough to send snow from the tree boughs in puffs of white.

Jeremy wrapped his arm around Isabel. "Can I tell you a secret?"

Truly, the question could have easily been her own. "You can tell me anything."

"I'm so happy right now."

A heavy sigh left her lips, equal parts contentment and worry. "Me, too," she replied, hoping against hope that this happiness would last.

Twelve

Isabel's worries about being pregnant had manifested themselves in some very specific dreams. The truly odd part was that they were still lingering, at least in her head. Half-awake with her eyes still shut, she heard tiny cries—baby wails so peculiar they didn't sound human.

"The kittens." She bolted upright, blinking in the early light of Jeremy's bedroom. She reached over and shook his arm. "Jeremy. I think Cat had her babies."

"What?" He managed to make disorientation adorable, lifting his head off the pillow, then plopping it back down. "We don't have to do anything, right? You told me she can take care of them on her own."

Typical guy. "We don't have to do anything, but

don't you want to make sure she's okay? That the babies are okay?" She tore back the comforter and tiptoed over to the closet door, turning on the light. She wasn't too worried about scaring Cat or the babies—it was plenty dark in their little corner. "Don't you want to see how many there are? Or what they look like?"

"Oh. Uh. Sure." He sat up in bed and flipped on the light on his bedside table, pushing his sexy bedhead hair off his face. "I'm coming."

Isabel tiptoed into the closet and pulled back Jeremy's shirts, peeking down into the box. Suckling Cat's belly were two tiny kittens; both appeared to be orange, although their fur was still matted. A third, with orange, gray and white patches, was blindly wandering around the box, crawling on its belly and mewing. Cat looked completely spent, asleep on her side.

"I thought they would be cuter," Jeremy said, peering over Isabel's shoulder. "Kittens are supposed to be cute."

Isabel shook her head and looked back at him. "Not at first. Not really. They'll be plenty cute in a few days."

"I'll have to trust you on that one."

He consulted his Apple watch. "It's nearly seven thirty, which seems way too early a time to be up on a Sunday morning, but I guess we're up, huh? Should I go make coffee?"

"That would be great. Bring me a cup?" She made herself at home on the floor, right next to the box.

"Are we spending our whole day in the closet?"

"I just want to sit here a little while. Make sure they're doing okay before we leave Cat to it."

He leaned down and pecked the top of her head. "I will not begrudge you your kitten time."

Isabel turned her attention to the box, watching as the stray kitten finally found her way to Cat's belly. It had been a long time since she'd been around this scene. She'd been a teenager the last time their family had newborn kittens in the house. Even all these years later, witnessing this made her feel connected to her mom. She pressed her hand to her lower belly, wondering what her body would ultimately tell her. She'd have been lying if she said she didn't desperately want a baby and to become a mom. But she wanted it all—true love and a partner. She would do this on her own, but it wasn't what her heart desired.

Jeremy returned and handed her a cup of coffee. "Good?" he asked, distracted by his iPad.

"Yes. Perfect." It was prepared exactly the way she liked it, with a splash of cream and one sugar.

"Good. Because here's where I have to ruin your day. There's a story in the paper this morning. Apparently somebody found love letters written to Victoria Eden by Mr. Summers's father. And the papers decided to publish them."

Isabel felt all of the blood drain from her face. *No no no.* She scrambled to standing and took the tablet from Jeremy when he offered it to her. There in black and white were the letters she and Mindy had discovered that afternoon in her grandmother's apartment. They had agreed to hide them away. They had agreed that no good came of anyone seeing them.

"How did you find out about this?" She felt her entire body go tight, fearing the answer.

"Summers, of course. Nothing gets past that guy. He texted me a link and asked me to call him, but I wanted to talk to you first. What the hell, Isabel? I thought we had a deal. I thought we were putting this whole thing to rest."

"We *do* have a deal." She hated seeing the expression on his face—the sheer disappointment was excruciating. Meanwhile, her mind was racing, wondering how this could have possibly happened. "Why are you looking at me like that? I didn't do this."

"Your clients must have done it. There's no other explanation." He took the tablet from her hand and stalked out of the closet.

She followed him back into his room. "But that doesn't make any sense. Why would they do this? Especially when I specifically asked Mindy not to?"

The look on Jeremy's face when he turned around told her what a grave error she'd made. She'd grown so comfortable with him that she'd let down her guard. He didn't know about the letters. She'd never said a peep about them, not even after he'd called to let her know that the promissory note had been authenticated. "Please tell me you didn't plan this. Please tell me this isn't a trademark Isabel Blackwell move."

That stung like no other thing he could have said. "Jeremy, no. I didn't plan this. I don't know what to tell you, but I didn't have anything to do with this story."

"Did you know about the letters?"

A sigh left her lips involuntarily and he stormed out of the room. "Jeremy, wait!" She ran out into the hall after him, grabbing his arm just as he reached the top of the landing. "Please let me explain. Yes, I knew about the letters. Mindy and I found them right before the promissory note was authenticated."

"But you still waited for me to call you and tell you about the authentication. Even when you knew at that point that it was all real? The affair between Mr. Summers's father and Victoria Eden was real?"

"Of course I waited. You would have done the same thing in my situation."

He closed his eyes and pinched the bridge of his nose, not saying a thing.

"You would have. You know it."

"Of course I would have, Isabel. My first duty is to my client. Which only illustrates how far you and I have crossed the line together. And now I have feelings for you and what in the hell am I supposed to do about that?"

She sharply sucked in a breath. "Feelings?" She had feelings for him, too, but she didn't have the nerve to express them now. The thought of sitting down and examining them, or daring to put a label on them, was too terrifying an idea. Meanwhile, there was no sign of her period and the drugstore was scheduled to deliver a pregnancy test at any time.

"Please don't throw my word back at me like I've said something horrible. We've had a great weekend together and now we're right back where we started except that it's quite possibly worse. I don't see any way that Summers is going to agree to a single term you and I so carefully worked out. The entire deal is off as far as I'm concerned."

Isabel's stomach sank. She'd not only disappointed Jeremy, she was about to crush the entire Eden family and her brother, for that matter. Best-case scenario, Eden's would end up embroiled in a legal battle for months, one that would cost them untold sums of money. Mr. Summers had been headed for the warpath from the very beginning and it was only understandable that this story in the papers would convince him it was the only course. Mindy and Isabel had found the letters extremely romantic when they read them, but there was no doubt that they were the flowery ramblings of a man smitten with a woman who was not his wife. They were a chronicle of lust, passion, obsession and ultimately, infidelity. They told the story of two people casting aside the sanctity of marriage.

"Please. Let me talk to Mindy and Sophie. Let me get to the bottom of this."

"I don't see what good it's going to do, but I'm not going to prevent you from doing whatever you need to do to take care of your client."

"Gee, thanks. That's so generous of you." Isabel retreated to the guest room, fuming and upset and uncharacteristically on the brink of tears. Normally when things went wrong with a case, she immediately went on the offensive. Right now, she wanted to crumple into a ball and hide. She got out her phone and called her brother.

"Hey. What's up?" he asked, sounding as though he was still recovering from his cold.

"Have you seen the papers?"

"No. Why?"

Isabel gave Sam a quick recap. "So I need to know if Mindy fed this story to the newspapers."

"I don't see how she possibly could have. At least not in the last few days. She's been completely out of it on cold medicine. The only person she's talked to has been Sophie."

Isabel felt like a light bulb had been flicked on above her head. Sophie was the most likely person to do something like this. When Isabel had tried to calm her down the other morning, she was all ready to hire a PR person and take Mr. Summers down. "Okay. Thanks. I need to call her and talk to her."

"Are we in hot water because of this?" Sam asked.

Isabel wasn't about to couch it. "I'd say we're about to boil."

Unfortunately, when Isabel called Sophie's cell, all she got was voice mail. She left a message, asking—no, begging—for Sophie to call her back. Then she flopped back on the bed and stared up at the ceiling, wondering how she was possibly ever going to get herself out of this.

Jeremy had sought the solitude of his office, closing the door behind him. He wasn't interested in Isabel's excuses or reasoning. All he could think about were the things he'd learned about her the first time he'd looked into her career trajectory and discovered what she'd done in Washington, DC. This was straight out of the Isabel Blackwell playbook—when one party can destroy you, you destroy them first. Although he didn't want to make this situation about him, this was far too much like the things Kelsey had done to him. His heart legitimately went out to Mr. Summers. Who wants to read a newspaper article where their father, in his own words, professes his love for someone who isn't his wife?

He couldn't believe he'd fallen back into bed with Isabel. He couldn't believe he'd let himself get so carried away again. Even five minutes ago out in the hall with her—why had he uttered that word? *Feelings?* For someone who was supposed to be exceptionally good with words, he'd sure chosen a terrible one. Right now, he had a few too many feelings coursing through his system, anger being pretty high on the list. Everyone was pissing him off—the Eden sisters, the situation and honestly, even Isabel.

Jeremy's phone, which was facedown on his desk, beeped with a text. Then another. He flipped over the device and scanned the screen.

The first message was from his father. Summers case is no longer under your control. We need to take down Blackwell.

The second was from a reporter, and just because today seemed to be hell-bent on destroying him, it was the same one who'd sought Jeremy's comment after Kelsey ran her smear piece. Can we talk re: the Benjamin Summers lawsuit?

Before he spoke to either of those people, he needed to call Ben. He didn't want to risk him talking to his father first. "Ben. Good morning. I got your text," Jeremy said, wanting to be as upbeat and diplomatic as possible, even though it felt like the world was crumbling around him.

"It appears that the shoe is on the other foot, doesn't it? I'm embarrassed beyond words at the atrocity in the papers this morning, but I suppose I should be thankful that the Eden's team has finally shown their true colors."

"I don't know about that. We're still trying to get to the bottom of exactly what happened." Why was it his inclination to try to walk any of this back? Logic said that he should be going for the jugular right now, but the truth was that he just wanted this done. He couldn't spend more time with Isabel. She'd shown that she was just as capable of inflicting damage as any woman he'd ever allowed himself to get close to. He needed this case to be over. "I have to tell you that Ms. Blackwell and I worked out some extremely favorable terms for you on Friday. It's an attractive offer, and yes, today might give us additional leverage for perhaps a few more concessions, but I don't think we should throw the whole thing out the window because of one story in a tabloid."

"And I'd think you would be happy about this. Don't lawyers love leverage?"

"Not when it means that we needlessly drag something out for longer than it needs to go." He could see this going on for months and months, during which he would have to battle Isabel. He didn't want that. Frankly, he wanted this whole thing to go away so he could decide for himself, without any outside intrusion, whether he could trust her. Whether they could be something.

"Do you have these supposed favorable terms for me to look at?" Mr. Summers asked.

"I'm in the process of drawing them up. We can meet tomorrow morning if that works for you."

"Fine. Nine o'clock. My office."

"Absolutely. I will be there."

"And if I'm not happy, I'm prepared to drop the gloves and go to war." The line went dead before Jeremy had a chance to respond. Not that he had anything to say. He'd wait until tomorrow to do battle with Mr. Summers.

Of course, now he had no choice but to call his dad and explain what was going on. As the phone rang, dread began to build in his system, and all Jeremy could think was that this entire situation was wrong, starting with the fact that he couldn't stand to speak to a man he should have been able to trust and confide in—his own father.

"I just got off the phone with Mr. Summers," Jeremy started. "We're meeting tomorrow morning. I'm presenting the terms of the negotiation to him. I'm hoping he can put aside what happened in the papers today and agree to everything. He'll get his money. He'll get that and more."

"That's not even my worry anymore, Jeremy. My concern is that you have caused irreparable damage to our firm's reputation. You're making us look like a bunch of hacks."

"Dad. I'm not a public relations guy. I have no control over what runs in the newspaper."

"But if you had put this case to bed at that first meeting, if you had the nerve to be ruthless with Ms. Blackwell, we wouldn't be having this discussion."

"It wouldn't have changed the tabloid story. That still could have run."

"And Summers would have had his settlement by then. At that point, Sharp and Sharp would only be bandied about as the firm who had come out on top. Instead, we're flopping around like a fish out of water." His father cleared his throat. "I think I need to level the playing field."

"By doing what exactly?"

"We need to get rid of Ms. Blackwell. Get Eden's to fire her."

"They won't fire her. Her brother is engaged to Mindy Eden. He's a special adviser to the store."

Jeremy couldn't explain further, about how Isabel felt like she was part of the Eden family and how it all meant a great deal to her. He couldn't divulge his personal involvement with her. It would infuriate his father to no end, and Jeremy had to admit, he would be justified in being angry.

"Trust me, they'll get rid of her when she's a liability, and I know exactly how to make that happen. Then they'll hand it over to their in-house counsel. You can steamroller those guys in your sleep."

"Dad. Please don't do anything reckless. Just let me meet with Summers tomorrow morning and see where we get. Just give me this one last chance."

Thirteen

Monday morning had arrived, which meant it was do-or-die time. Jeremy would be leaving the house in a half hour to meet with Mr. Summers. He hoped that Ben had taken some time to cool off. He hoped that he could see that there was no point in letting pride get in the way. It was time for an agreement. An armistice. That was the best-case scenario for Jeremy and he wanted it so badly he could taste it.

Sunday had been horrible—Jeremy stewing in his office and Isabel in the guest room, tucked away. Their only real interaction came when she got a delivery and he brought it to her room.

"This came from the drugstore." He handed her

the paper shopping bag, hating that he felt as though he had to stay out of a room in his own house.

"Thank you," she said, clutching it to her chest. "I got a call from the Bacharach and I can move back in on Tuesday morning. If you want, I can see if Mindy and Sam can take me in. Or maybe I could stay in Mindy's grandmother's old apartment."

"Don't do that. Just stay. It's fine." He desperately wanted that to be true. It was killing him to not be where they'd been mere hours before that, enjoying each other's company, touching each other, kissing.

"I know this story just made everything worse. And I'm really sorry for that. I still don't know what happened, but I will get to the bottom of it. I wish I had something you could tell Mr. Summers, but I don't."

"Okay. I still plan to meet with him tomorrow morning. No telling what he's going to say, but I will present our agreement to him if you still want me to."

Isabel had picked at her fingernail, seeming to want any reason to not look at him. "I'll do the same and I guess we'll just see where we end up?"

He nodded in agreement. "Do you want something to eat?"

She shook her head. "Not right now. Maybe later. I'm tired and I have work to do."

"Okay then. Let me know if you need anything." He'd been about to walk away when she said one more thing.

"I checked on the kittens while you were in your

office. I made sure Cat got some food and water. They seem like they're doing well."

"Good. Thank you."

"Of course."

With that, she'd shut the door, and Jeremy was left much like he'd been before Isabel had arrived on his doorstep—alone. It stayed like that for the rest of the day. And the night. And for all of that morning.

In his closet, he was choosing a suit to wear for his meeting with Mr. Summers when he heard one of the kittens mewing. In all of the commotion of yesterday, he'd frankly forgotten that they were there. The two orange kittens were nursing, but the other one was wandering around the box, bumping into the sides. Cat would nudge at her with her nose occasionally, but the kitten, quite frankly, seemed lost. Jeremy was unsure of what to do, but something told him he had to help the poor thing, so he reached in, picked it up and placed her next to her siblings, mouth near Cat's belly. He watched as she rooted around and latched on to nurse. There was some consolation in that one silly achievement—today wouldn't have to be a total loss.

After dressing, he went into his office to gather his things. That was when Isabel appeared at his door. She was just as beautiful as always, but he could tell that there was something on her mind. She wasn't her normal lively self, and the dread that prompted in him made him sick to his stomach.

"Do you have a minute?" she asked. "I have two things I need to talk to you about."

"Sure. I have to leave soon, but I'll always make time for you."

"First off, you should know that your dad tried to get one of the tabloids to run a smear piece on me. The reporter called me late last night for comment and after I spoke to the editor, they agreed not to run it."

Jeremy looked up at the ceiling, furious with his father for attempting to sabotage her while also relieved that he hadn't been successful. "I'm so sorry. I don't know what to say."

She waved it off. "Don't worry. I've had worse things happen to me. And I'm sure that whatever they wanted to print would probably be true. I've represented some people who aren't great. But I've always acted in accordance with the law. I don't have anything I'm ashamed of."

"Well, good. I'm glad."

"I simply don't want to be a part of any of this anymore. I can't deal with the mudslinging and the backstabbing and everyone trying so hard to disparage each other. I'm hoping we can wrap up the case, but if we can't, I think I will likely step away from it. I've had my fill of it. I love the Eden sisters and care about them deeply, but I also need my sanity."

"I can't say that I blame you. If my dad wasn't in the middle of it, I might be tempted to bail on Summers. None of this has been very fun, has it?"

She shrugged and a slight smile crossed her lips. It was like stepping into the sunlight for the first time—that small glimmer of happiness from her made everything better. "I don't know about that. I had fun with you. I had more than fun."

A grin that he was sure was quite goofy broke out on his face. "Me, too. I don't regret that part."

"Me, either. Which brings me to the other thing I have to tell you. There's no easy way to say this, so I'm just going to come out with it. I'm pregnant and you're the father."

Of the many things Jeremy had thought Isabel might tell him, that one piece of information had never occurred to him. Not even for a second. "The night we met?"

"Yes."

"But you…"

"I know. I thought there was no chance. I was wrong."

"I, uh… I don't even know what to say."

"I know. It's okay. You don't need to say anything. This is all very sudden and it's a lot to deal with, especially given everything else that's going on." Now that she was talking, she was picking up speed, as if she had a long list of things she'd been dying to say. "I realize that the timing couldn't possibly be any worse. And we don't really know each other that well, so I understand that you would be wanting to distance yourself from me, and I can appreciate why.

It's okay. I will be completely fine on my own. I don't want you to worry."

He got up from his desk and went to her, taking her hands. "Hey. Hey. Slow down a minute. Take a breath."

She dropped her head for a moment and when she looked up at him, there were tears rolling down her cheeks. "I've wanted a baby for so long, Jeremy. I've always wanted to be a mom. But this isn't the way I wanted it to happen. And I hate putting you on the spot. You're a good man. I know that. You're sweet and generous and you don't deserve to be in this situation."

Jeremy wasn't sure what to think about any of this. He'd wanted a family for a long time. He'd wanted a woman like Isabel for a long time. But this was traveling on a preposterous timeline. He wanted to put the entire world on pause, if only for a day so he could have time and space to think. A baby? With Isabel? How would this work? Would it be yet another negotiation? That was the last thing he wanted. And what if things didn't work out? He didn't want to be an absentee father, around every other weekend and select holidays. That wasn't what he wanted for himself at all. It wasn't what he wanted for Isabel, either.

His phone beeped—the reminder that he had to leave for his meeting. "Shoot. I'm going to be late to meet with Summers. He's such a stickler for punctuality. I can't afford to make him angry."

"I understand. It's okay. Just forget what I said. We can talk about it after everything with the case is over."

Jeremy grabbed his briefcase from his desk, then returned to her. "Hey. Will you stop trying to let me off the hook? I'm not like that guy who burned you. I don't turn my back on people who need me, okay? So just give me a chance to meet with Summers, and talk to my dad, and, and…" He looked at her, certain he couldn't possibly be in a bigger state of disbelief. "Then we'll talk about the baby."

That fresh start Isabel had wanted so badly? It felt like she was watching it crumble to dust in her hands. How could she possibly save Eden's now? How could Jeremy salvage this situation for Mr. Summers? Even more important, how could the two of them reach an understanding about impending parenthood? They'd hardly had enough time to fall in love.

The scene in the guest bath at Jeremy's house was still rolling around in her mind. She'd paced back and forth across the white marble floor, arms wrapped around her middle like she was giving herself a hug. She'd been unable to escape how lonely it felt to be doing that on her own, for the second time. It had played out like that when she found out she was pregnant with Garrett's baby all those years ago—Isabel enduring the painfully slow ticks of the clock while she waited for news that could change her whole life.

The timer on Isabel's phone had gone off, echoing in the bathroom. She'd closed her eyes for a moment to steel herself for the news, unable to decide what result she hoped for, although she'd known that there was no reason to reach a solid conclusion. Her heart would tell her with its own reaction.

She'd opened her eyes and grabbed the test from the counter. *Two blue lines. Positive.* She'd stumbled back into the bathroom wall, steadying herself with her hand. *Positive. A baby.* Her heart did the inexplicable, even when her stomach wobbled—it began to flutter in her chest. However imperfect her situation, a baby was something she wanted more than anything. She'd been waiting years for another chance.

She had to admit to herself that Jeremy had handled the news far better than expected. She'd been prepared for the absolute worst, and he'd kept everything on an even keel. He'd been a rock. She hoped and prayed that this wasn't another of his acting jobs. She didn't think she could take it if he wasn't at least going to play some role in this baby's life. She couldn't handle it if he was going to turn his back on her as Garrett had done.

In the car on the way to Eden's to meet with Sam, Mindy, Sophie and Emma, her heart was heavy. Perhaps her first mistake had been taking this job— she'd only agreed out of loyalty to Sam. But now she was so much closer to Mindy, Sophie and Emma than she'd ever imagined she could be, and it was all on her that they could lose the store. Isabel the fixer had not only failed to fix anything, she'd allowed it to get worse. She should have had the sense to take the letters into her possession that day at Victoria Eden's apartment. She never should have trusted her clients to keep them out of public view.

Arriving at Eden's, she waved to Duane the security guard and marched right back to the elevator, prepared to unleash a few unpleasant things on the Eden sisters if necessary. If they'd gotten themselves into this mess, she wasn't sure she could get them out. She strode into the lobby feeling determined, but the instant she saw Sam, she burst into tears. He rushed over to her and gathered her up in his arms.

"What's wrong?" he asked. "Are you that upset about the case?"

She sank against his chest, unable to speak. As much as Eden's had weighed on her as recently as a few minutes ago, that was definitely not what was on her mind.

Mindy appeared in the reception area. "Is everything okay?" She stepped closer, but kept her distance. "Sorry. I'd hug you, but I'm still getting over this cold."

"Is Summers going to go after the store?" Sam asked.

"I still haven't talked to Sophie, but it has to be her," Mindy said. "I don't completely remember our conversation over the weekend, but I'm pretty sure I told her about the letters. Leave it to her to go to our grandmother's apartment, find them and leak them to the press."

Mindy's explanation was of little consolation. Isabel still felt as though she had let down her new friends. She'd let down their entire family. She'd let down Sam's wife-to-be. She'd failed in every way imaginable, at least when it came to her legal responsibilities. "I'm so sorry. I really wish I had better news. Summers is just out for revenge. I'm not sure we ever had a chance."

Sam placed his hands on Isabel's shoulders. "I know you did your best. Some of this has to be his lawyer. I didn't like Sharp from the very first meeting. He seems like a real weasel."

Isabel froze, looking up into her brother's eyes. Sam's opinion mattered. It mattered a lot. And she couldn't allow him to think of Jeremy that way. She also couldn't keep him in the dark any longer about the full scope of her relationship with him, especially now that it had become infinitely more complicated. "Jeremy's a good man. He's caught in an impossible situation. Summers is unreasonable."

"You have Stockholm syndrome. You were stuck negotiating with that guy. You've convinced yourself he's not that bad."

"I don't know about that," Mindy said.

Sam turned to her. "Don't you agree?" he asked.

"For Isabel's sake, I can't. If she says he's a good guy, I believe her."

"Why? This guy is about to destroy your entire family."

"He's not going to destroy our family. He might

end up being part and parcel of ending our business, but it's not the same."

"Wait a minute. Why do I have the feeling you two have talked about him before?" Sam asked. "Am I missing something?"

"We did talk about him. The day we rummaged around in Gram's apartment."

Isabel had fond memories of that day, despite the things they'd discovered. She felt closer to Mindy afterward. She felt as though she was becoming part of the Eden family. "We talked about a lot that day." Isabel loved her brother deeply, and it was time to tell him and Mindy everything. "I need to tell you both something. There's more going on than just the negotiations breaking down. Jeremy and I are involved," Isabel whispered.

It wasn't easy to take Sam by surprise, but he noticeably reared back his head. "Are you serious? Why would you do that? That's so unprofessional."

Mindy grabbed both of their arms. "You two. In my office. We can't have this conversation out here."

As soon as they were behind a closed door, Isabel confronted Sam. "You're going to lecture me about professionalism? Seriously? I didn't even want this job to begin with."

"Wait. You didn't?" Mindy asked, incredulous. "I thought you did. Sam, you told me she wanted to help us."

"She took the job. That was all you needed to know."

Mindy let out a frustrated grumble. "You can't keep things like this from me. Isabel is going to be my sister-in-law. We've been getting along great and now I find out that the foundation of that is all a lie."

Isabel reached for Mindy's arm. "It's not a lie. As soon as we spent that afternoon together, I knew I was doing the right thing. I wanted to help you and your sisters. I wanted us to be close. That's why I told you about my thing with Jer…" Isabel stopped herself, but it was too late.

"Whoa. Hold on a minute. You were involved with Jeremy before? I'm so confused. And Min, you knew about this?"

Isabel couldn't allow Mindy to take heat for this, so she explained that she and Jeremy had a one-night stand before they were involved in the case. Then she told him about the broken condom.

Sam shook his head, holding up both hands. "Enough. I don't need to hear about that." He closed his eyes and pinched the bridge of his nose. "So when we met him in his office that day, you guys had already slept together? And you didn't say a thing to any of us."

"What was I supposed to do? He had his client and I had mine and none of that was going to change the fact that there was this case standing between us."

"And now what? Where do you two stand?" Sam asked.

Isabel knew she had to come clean. About everything. "I got pregnant that first night. With Jeremy's baby. I found out this morning."

Sam walked over and sat on the couch, but Mindy went straight to Isabel.

"Oh my God. Are you okay?" she asked.

Isabel had to take a moment to reflect. Was she okay? "I am. I mean, I've wanted to have a baby for a long time now. Ever since…" There were far too many details of her life she had kept from Sam. Perhaps it had been Isabel's way of protecting him. With both of their parents gone and Isabel being two years older, she certainly felt responsible for him.

"Ever since what?" Sam asked, seeming desperate. "Just tell me what's going on, Isabel. I feel like I am completely in the dark, which is not a good feeling when it comes to my own sister."

Apparently that day was for nothing but revelations and admissions. So she finally told Sam about the heartache of losing her first pregnancy, and how she so desperately wanted this child.

"What are you going to do?" he asked when she'd told him everything.

"Right now, all I can do is my best for me and the baby. I have absolutely no idea what's going to happen with any of it. The deal or Jeremy."

Fourteen

Jeremy left his meeting with Mr. Summers feeling as though he'd been hit by a truck. The man's ability to hold on to a grudge and to allow every perceived slight to fester…well, it was unparalleled.

Nothing had been resolved, but Mr. Summers promised him a phone call in an hour with an answer. Either he would accept the terms from the Eden's team or it would be all-out war. Which left Jeremy with one more thing to deal with—his dad. No matter what happened with the case, he was done.

He headed straight to the office and didn't even stop to drop off his things. "I need to speak to my father," he said to his dad's admin, striding right past her desk and opening the door. "I heard that your plan to smear Ms. Blackwell didn't work. I guess I should be thankful you failed."

Jeremy's dad was on a call. "I'm gong to have to call you back," he said into the receiver before hanging up. "I can still make it happen. I just need to dig up more dirt on her."

"Just don't. Just stop all of this. You're as bad as Mr. Summers. There is no winning when you play the game like this. It's just a race to the bottom and I'm tired of it."

"You're complaining about your boss and your biggest client. Apparently you don't know who signs your paychecks."

"Don't posture with me, Dad. You know that the other lawyers and I are the ones who keep the lights on. You're just the head of the dragon, spitting fire and still trying to prove yourself because you know that no matter how hard you try, you will never be as good as your own dad."

"That's not true. The success of this firm begins and ends with me. It's my legacy."

That word didn't sit right with Jeremy. "I'm your son. Am I not your real legacy? The firm could go under tomorrow and I would still be here, trying to find a way to make you happy. Trying to find a way to get through to you."

Just then, the door to his father's office opened and in walked the last person he expected to see— his mother. "Jeremy. I thought it was strange that you weren't at your desk."

"Mom. What are you doing here?"

"Trying to get your father to go Christmas shopping with me."

"I'm in the middle of something," his dad said. "I can't drop everything and go shopping."

"Why not?" Jeremy asked. "Everything is under control here. The other lawyers and I have everything in hand."

"The Summers case isn't resolved."

"No, it isn't. But it will be. And I'll see it through."

"Then what?" his dad asked. "You'll get another client I have to bother you about?"

"You never had to bother me about this one. If you trusted me to do my job, it would get done. Grandpa trusted you. I don't know why you can't place that same faith in me." Jeremy stuffed his hands into his pants pockets, frustrated.

His mother turned to him. "Your grandfather never trusted him. Your dad was proving himself until the day his father died. He never had a chance to win his confidence."

Jeremy was frozen for a moment, letting that bit of information tumble around in his head. "What? Seriously?"

His dad drew in a deep breath, staring off into space as if he couldn't possibly handle the admission. "He never made things easy on me. That's for sure."

Jeremy's mom stepped closer to him. "As the person who had to listen to your father complain every night when he came home from work, I can tell you that it was far worse than that."

"Dad? Why didn't you ever tell me this? And why are you doing the same thing to me?"

"Because it made me stronger to be tested like that," his dad snapped. "It made me a better lawyer."

Jeremy wanted to laugh, but this was all striking him as incredibly sad. If only they'd had this conversation ten or fifteen years ago. He might be in a very different place. "You don't have to be miserable to be strong. That all comes from within as far as I'm concerned."

"It's the only way I know, Jeremy. I don't know what you want me to tell you."

Jeremy approached his dad's desk. "Dad. I love you. I hope you know that. I love you even though you make it very difficult some days. But I can't work with you anymore. Either you step aside or I do. I'll leave it up to you."

His mom came up behind him. "Son. Do you really want to do that? Close this door on your career?"

He turned to her and placed his hand on her arm. He really did love her. "My career isn't going anywhere. But at the rate we're going, the three of us aren't going to be much of a family. The situation at work has been bad enough, but we need to talk about how things went south after Kelsey left me. I didn't feel supported. And I never took the time to think about how unhappy it made me until I talked to a friend about it." Isabel had shown him so much in such a short amount of time. How had she done that?

"You never told us you felt that way. I thought we were supportive."

"I should have said something. I know that now. I shouldn't have kept it bottled in. But you were not supportive. You were embarrassed."

"Embarrassed for you. The things Kelsey said about you were horrible. No mother wants her son to go through that. To experience that kind of betrayal."

"But you never really said those things to me. All I heard were the things your friends were telling you."

Jeremy's mom frowned and her eyes grew misty. "I didn't?"

He shook his head. "You didn't."

She wrapped her arms around him. "I'm so sorry. I never, ever wanted to hurt you. You and your father are the most important things to me in the entire world. I love you. I love you both."

Jeremy returned his mom's hug. "I love you guys, too. Hopefully that can save us." As soon as the words left his lips, he realized that they weren't really his. They were Isabel's. From the night they met. *I believe that love is the only thing that saves anyone.*

The thought of Isabel sent goose bumps racing over the surface of his skin and that was when he realized it—he loved her. As improbable as it was, he'd fallen in love with her. Could love save him? Was it as simple as that? Was it meant for him? He'd spent the last few years so unhappy, convinced that his empty existence was something he must learn to accept. A fact of life. But did it really have to be that way? He wanted to believe that it didn't.

"Are we going to see you for the tree-trimming party?" his mom asked. "I look forward to it all year."

Jeremy was determined to keep building bridges, not tearing them down. He wanted to be the sort of man who made connections, not destroyed them. "My only problem is that I'd like to bring a date. Isabel Blackwell."

His dad's eyes became as large as dinner plates. "Excuse me?"

Jeremy wasn't about to go into a long, drawn-out explanation. He wasn't even certain Isabel would accept the invitation. "Yes, Dad. We actually had a brief romantic relationship before the case started. I never said anything because I thought it wouldn't be a problem. And honestly, it wasn't, until you decided to try to drag her through the mud today."

Jeremy's mother's face was full of horror. "Oh. Well, that's awkward, isn't it?"

Honestly, it couldn't be any more uncomfortable for Jeremy than anything else he'd endured with his parents. "It doesn't have to be if Dad apologizes."

"You have to apologize," his mother blurted. "Otherwise, it'll ruin Christmas."

"You can't ruin Christmas, Dad."

Full of resignation, his father nodded. "I will apologize. First thing."

Jeremy could be content with that. "Then I will do my best to convince her to come."

Jeremy said his goodbyes to his parents, then marched down the hall, feeling as though a weight had been lifted. He'd finally said his piece with his family and the world hadn't ended. In fact, it had gone quite well.

Just then, his phone rang. He plucked it from his pocket and answered, striding down the hall.

"Yes?"

"Jeremy. It's Ben."

At this point, Jeremy was prepared for anything. "Do you have news for me?"

"I do."

"Am I going to be happy about it?"

"Depends on what you were hoping for."

Was Jeremy ready for the answer? He had to be. Because the truth was that he wanted to put this whole thing to bed and turn his attention to Isabel and the baby.

Isabel arrived back at Jeremy's place, and of course, it just *had* to be snowing. Again. As if the sight of his beautiful brownstone, with the grand steps and stunning front door, didn't hold enough vibrant reminders of what had happened between them. They'd not only fallen into bed, she'd fallen into the Christmas spirit for the first time in years.

Funnily enough, the most pressing thing she could think of as she looked at the facade of Jeremy's house was that it needed a wreath with a big fat red bow. She needed to rein herself in. There was no telling what that afternoon might hold. Jeremy was having a showdown with his father and Mr. Summers. There were too many things that could go wrong.

As she climbed out of the car and zipped up her coat, she had to admit to herself that despite her predicament, she wasn't feeling truly pessimistic right now. She accepted the reality of her situation. Jeremy had never asked for this—an undeniable tie to her, forever. And that was fine. She was strong and independent. She could care for a child on her own. And she'd wanted this more than anything for so long. Nothing was going to keep her from building her own little family. Life was once again proving to be quite unlike what she had hoped for, but she wouldn't put herself or her future on hold. She'd done that after Garrett left, and the pain of losing her first pregnancy had made her tread water for years.

But as she ascended his front steps, she was overcome with another wave of melancholy. She and Jeremy could be good together if they had a chance. They could be great. She cared for him deeply, and was holding on to feelings that sure felt an awful lot like love. Such was the case with bad timing. Only some things in life lined up perfectly. Not everything. At least not for Isabel.

She unlocked the door with the key Jeremy had given her and flipped on the light in the foyer. After taking off her coat, she made her way upstairs to check on Cat and the kittens.

"Hey there, Mama," she said when she carefully

pulled back Jeremy's dress shirts to reveal the cardboard box. Cat was half-asleep with her eyes part open, the kittens nursing and kneading at her belly. Cat looked up at Isabel and blinked—such a simple thing, and yet Isabel was so taken by the beauty of the moment. There was this sweet and beautiful creature caring for her babies, at utter peace with the world. Isabel hoped that her future could be like that.

She hoped more than was probably reasonable.

"Hello? Isabel?" Jeremy's voice came from downstairs. "Are you home?"

Home. She was home. She wanted to believe she was. "I'm up here. With the cats."

She heard his steady footfalls on the stairs and moments later, he appeared at the closet doorway. "Of course you're up here."

"I had to get my kitten time."

"I'm wondering if I can steal a minute with you. Or maybe more." From behind his back, he produced a huge bouquet of red roses. "I'm hoping these will convince you."

Isabel popped up from the floor, planted her face in the flowers and drew in the heavenly smell. "I don't need convincing to talk to you. Although I appreciate the effort. They're beautiful." She then worried there might be a specific reason for the kind gesture. "Mr. Summers. Did you talk to him? Is he throwing down the gauntlet?"

"I did talk to him. For quite a while, actually. Turns out that when he got so mad about the story yesterday, he hadn't actually read the letters. After I talked to him this morning, he finally did."

"And that made things better or worse?"

"Better. Much better. He called and told me that he realized just how much his father loved Victoria Eden. Truly loved her. I guess that in the end, he stopped seeing it as this salacious affair and more as a love story between two people who met at the wrong time."

Isabel blinked several times, struggling to catch up. "So what does that mean?"

"He's agreed to the terms. A lump sum of the original loan amount by January 1 and 10 percent of the Eden's online business in perpetuity." Jeremy shrugged his way out of his suit jacket and hung it on a hanger. "So I guess what I need to know from you is whether the Eden family is definitely on board."

"They are. I heard from Mindy on my way back here and it was Sophie who leaked the letters to the press. I told her that they had to agree to the terms if we had any chance of wrapping this up."

"See? What a shark you are."

"I'm not. I'm just like you, Jeremy. I wanted this to be over so we could deal with the real-life stuff that's sitting in front of us. I know that I unloaded a lot on you today, and I'm not trying to let you off the hook, but I do want you to know that there is no pressure from me. You can take all the time you want to think about this and decide what you want."

"I already know what I want."

Isabel was surprised by his quick response. She

only hoped that he wasn't going to say that he'd decided he didn't want her. "You do?"

"Yes. And it all came to me when I had it out with my dad this morning." He reached for Isabel's hand. "Come on. Let's go sit on the bed so I can tell you the whole story."

They traced into the bedroom and sat on the edge of the mattress. He held her hand the whole time he was recounting what had happened with his parents and how relieved he was to finally clear the air.

"I'm so glad it all worked out. But I'm still not sure how that helped you figure out what you want."

"I ended up telling my mom something you said the night we met."

Isabel narrowed her eyes in confusion. "Good Lord, Jeremy. What in the heck were you talking to your mom about?"

He laughed so hard that she could see his body relax. "Love. We were talking about love."

"I don't remember us discussing that. At all."

"When you were telling me your universal truths. You said that you believe that love is the only thing that ever saves anyone. And as soon as the words came out of my mouth, I realized that you saved me. You brought me back to life."

He reached out and smoothed her hair back and she peered up into his eyes, which were full of tenderness and love, the things she most craved. "If I did that, Jeremy, it was only because you make it easy. You're so pure of heart. It's impossible to not get caught up in that. To admire it."

"If that's the case, it's because I'm better when I'm with you. That's all there is to it. And I don't want to walk away from what's already between us."

Isabel's mind raced. She felt the same way. Exactly. And it was only leaving her with one conclusion.

He sucked in a deep breath and blew it out. "It might sound crazy…"

Oh my God.

"I know we've only known each other for a little while…" he continued.

"But I love you." They both said it. At the exact same time.

For a moment, they sat there, staring at each other in disbelief. Then the laughter came and an embrace and finally a kiss that made every bad thing that had ever happened fade into nothingness. Isabel had waited her whole life for this moment, and she knew Jeremy had, too.

"The baby," she said. "I know it's a lot."

"Of course it's a lot. But I'm forty years old. I don't want to let life pass me by. I don't want to let you or this moment pass me by. We have to take everything life has given us here, Isabel."

"We have to take each other."

"Yes. Absolutely."

"And never let go."

Epilogue

"Do you think it's cheesy to get married on Valentine's Day?" Mindy posed the question to Isabel as they stood in the grand master bedroom of Sam and Mindy's splendid new home.

Isabel shook her head, helping her future sister-in-law adjust the bustle of her wedding gown. It was a jaw-dropping bias-cut silk charmeuse that hugged every curve. Isabel was guessing Sam might pass out the minute he saw her. "No. I think it's sweet."

"It was Sam's idea, you know. Who knew he could be such a sap?"

"I knew. I knew it all along." Isabel already found herself blinking away tears. It would be a miracle if she could get through the ceremony without sobbing.

Pregnancy hormones were definitely getting the best of her, but she relished every frantic and slightly chaotic moment of it. She'd be twelve weeks along in six days, then she and Jeremy would finally tell his parents. It'd been a bit of a rocky road to start with them, but they were making strides, especially since Jeremy's dad had apologized for trying to drag Isabel through the mud.

"How are we doing in here?" Sophie ducked into the room with Emma at her side.

Emma, who was showing all five months of her pregnancy, clasped her hand over her mouth when she saw Mindy. "You look so gorgeous. Sam is going to freak."

"You do look amazing. But I figured you already knew that," Sophie said, wandering farther into the room.

Mindy shot her a look. "A bride still wants to hear it, you know."

Sophie sat on the edge of the bed, watching Mindy adjust her hair. "I'm still surprised you didn't opt for a big wedding, but I suppose you've always been a bit contrary."

"After Emma and Daniel got married at city hall, I started to see the wisdom of it," Mindy said. "Having something low-key means way less drama. Plus, Sam didn't want to wait any longer, and honestly, I didn't want to, either."

The question of not waiting for life to start was certainly on Isabel's mind. She and Jeremy hadn't discussed marriage aside from agreeing it was best for the baby if it happened eventually. It wasn't that she was expecting a grand proclamation of love, more that she just wanted that certainty in her life. If he didn't pop the question soon, she planned to do it herself.

Of course, Jeremy had a lot on his plate now that he'd convinced his father to retire and step aside. There were lots of changes afoot at Sharp and Sharp as a result, including Jeremy bringing Isabel on board to start a new family law division. It was not only a good move forward for the firm, it was a way to save on office space, and they agreed that it would make things much easier when the baby arrived. They would likely get a nanny, but they also wanted to be as hands-on as possible.

A knock came at the bedroom door. Reginald, Eden's creative director and by all accounts, the sisters' de facto uncle, poked his head inside. "Everybody decent?" He didn't wait for a response, waltzing into the room in a pink suit and black bowtie festooned with pink hearts.

"Reginald, Gram would have loved that outfit," Sophie said.

He took it for a spin. "You think?"

"Definitely."

Mindy glanced at the clock on the bedside table. "You guys should head out there and get your seats."

Sophie, Emma and Isabel descended on Mindy, giving hugs and the gentlest of kisses on the cheek so as not to mess up her makeup. Sophie in particular was getting extremely choked up by the moment. "I love you all so much. Emma, you're the light and joy of this family. You make everything better. Mindy, you're the one who manages to keep us all moving forward." She then turned to Isabel. "And Isabel, at this point, you're pretty much our sister. We love you, too, and not just for saving Eden's. You helped us preserve our grandmother's legacy."

Isabel was so overwhelmed with emotion as the four of them joined in a group hug. "This means a lot to me. I've always wanted sisters."

Reginald cleared his throat loudly. "What about the stand-in for the father of the bride?"

"Get over here." Mindy waved him into the fray, but he only stayed for a beat or two before getting them all on schedule.

"Ladies, I need you to clear out. I have a bride to escort to the altar."

Isabel, Sophie and Emma hurried down the hall and descended the grand staircase into the foyer where the chairs were assembled. It was a small gathering— a few people from Eden's, like Lizzie and her new boyfriend, and Duane, the security guard. There were some people from Sam's office and Mindy's company, as well.

Isabel ducked into the seat next to Jeremy. "Hi," she whispered, pecking him on the cheek.

He took her hand and smiled, but otherwise kept quiet. Honestly, he'd been a little on edge all day, but she tried not to read anything into it. They were happy together, but he was under a lot of pressure to keep Sharp and Sharp firing on all cylinders.

Soft music began to play and everyone's attention was drawn to the top of the staircase, where Mindy stood with Reginald. As they began to descend, step by step, Isabel couldn't help but turn to a different sight, that of her brother waiting for his bride. She and Sam had been through so much together, and it felt like both a miracle and a blessing that they'd each found love, that they'd both found professional fulfillment and that they were now living in the same city. Her heart swelled at the thought of him having the happiness he so richly deserved.

The ceremony was short and sweet, officiated by one of Sam's friends from college, who'd recently moved to New York from Boston to work with him. He'd been ordained online for exactly this occasion. As her brother took Mindy into his arms, she couldn't have kept the tears at bay if she'd wanted to. It was too beautiful a moment to believe. Jeremy held her hand tightly, not letting go, and she hoped that it meant that no matter life's ups and downs, he would stay by her side.

As soon as Mindy and Sam walked down the very short aisle, the music got louder and decidedly more upbeat. "Now we get to have a party," Mindy announced, grabbing a glass of champagne from a waiter who had appeared from the kitchen. "Let's get these chairs out of here for dancing."

Sam pulled Isabel aside and gave her a warm hug. "It means the world to me that you could be here for this."

"Are you kidding? I wouldn't miss it for the world."

He looked down at the platinum band now circling the ring finger on his left hand. "Did you ever think I'd get married? Be honest."

"I always knew it would happen. It just took finding the right woman."

He pulled her into another bear hug. "So, at some point, Mindy and I want to talk to you about a legal matter."

Isabel reared back her head. "Not something to do with Eden's again. I barely survived the last one."

"Not that. The store is just fine. It's the question of children. Mindy and I were talking and we're considering adoption."

This surprised Isabel. "Is something wrong?"

"No. We haven't even started trying yet. I just…" He looked around the room at this massive home he and Mindy now owned. "There's a lot of room here and there are a lot of children in the world who need a good home. I think we'd like to do both. Have our own kids and adopt."

"Yes. Of course, yes. I would love to help."

"So you'll take our case?"

"Don't be silly. Just try to keep me away."

Jeremy came up by her side and shook Sam's hand. "Congratulations. It's a big day."

"The best big day ever." Sam unleashed a toothy grin, then winked at Jeremy, which Isabel found odd but decided it was because he was goofy with love. "Now if you'll excuse me, I need to hunt down the bride."

Isabel and Jeremy held hands as they watched him disappear into the other room. "How long do you want to stay?" Jeremy asked.

"I guess I feel like we should stay for the whole thing. Is everything okay? You seem preoccupied." She didn't want to let paranoia get the best of her, but she couldn't escape the feeling that something was wrong.

"Everything is absolutely perfect. You know me. I always want to get you home."

Isabel fought a smile. "Well, if that's what you're getting after, I'm thinking we stay an hour, tops."

They ended up staying fifty minutes. Isabel was tired and they had quite a ride back to Brooklyn. Jeremy was quiet as they sat in the back seat of the town car.

"You sure everything's okay?" she asked for what felt like the one hundredth time.

"Yeah. I spoke to my dad today. You know how that goes. It's getting better, but I still feel like I'm feeling my way around in the dark."

"Talk about work stuff?"

He nodded. "And just trying to get to a point where I have a better relationship with him. I went ahead and asked them about dinner next week. So we can tell them about the baby."

"And?"

He smiled. "Obviously I didn't tell them that part. But yes, they said that they would love to have dinner. My mom really adores you. She says you're good for me."

Isabel squeezed his hand tight. "Somebody needs to tell her that you're good for me."

They arrived back at Jeremy's and performed their new coming-home ritual, which was checking on the kittens. Jeremy, never the big cat fan, conceded that he had "warmed" to them. Of course, Isabel was over the moon for them, and the thought of them being adopted out soon weighed heavy on her heart. They wouldn't have this fun to look forward to much longer.

Isabel sat on the floor of the guest room and played with the three kittens, who still didn't have names. For now, they were Things 1, 2 and 3—the orange male, the orange female and the calico respectively. Jeremy, however, excused himself and said he needed to get something. That only left Isabel to worry about what his dad had said and how that played into the future of their relationship.

"What do you think, Thing 1?" Isabel scooped up the kitten and kissed him on the nose. The cat squirmed to get down and frolic with his littermates. In the corner, Cat was watching over everything. "Is Jeremy acting strangely?" Isabel asked Cat.

"I don't know. Am I?" Behind her, Jeremy had walked into the room.

Isabel turned quickly. "Whoa. You are stealthy. I didn't even hear you open the door."

"I think that's only because you're so wrapped up in the kittens."

She returned her attention to them as they wrestled on the carpet. "I do adore them. I love them."

Just then Jeremy knelt down next to her. "Do you know who I adore and love?"

She eyed him with great suspicion. "Okay, now you are definitely acting weird."

"You, Isabel. I love and adore you." He reached into the pocket of his pants and pulled out a small velvet bag. "And the reason I've been quiet all night is because I have a big question on my mind."

Isabel sat perfectly still, her heart beating unevenly in her chest. She didn't want to miss a moment or a single word of what she hoped was about to happen.

He reached for her hand and held on to it tightly. His gaze met hers, and she saw exactly how sincere he was. The hurt that she'd once seen in his eyes was gone. And now, she saw hope. "I love you, Isabel Blackwell, and it's not just because you're brilliant or beautiful. And it's not merely because you're having my baby, although that's part of it. I love you because you make my whole life better. I want you to be my wife." With that, he let go of her hand and opened the velvet bag, presenting a beautiful gold-

and-diamond solitaire. "This is why I talked to my dad. It's the ring my grandfather gave to my grandmother. He gave it to my dad, but my dad gave a different ring to my mom. He always felt bad about it, and I can't help but feel like this is all coming full circle now. As long as you'll say yes."

She had to laugh, at least a little bit, even as the tears streamed down her cheeks. "Of course the answer is yes. I love you, Jeremy. I love you for being strong and sensitive. I love you for not giving up on people. I love you for the way you make me feel like I'm the most important woman in the entire world."

"You *are* the most important woman in the world. No doubt about that." He leaned forward and kissed her, softly and sweetly, with just enough of that sexy Jeremy edge. She combed her fingers into his hair, wanting more.

Unfortunately, the kittens had different plans, tumbling around on the floor between them. In the excitement, Jeremy had dropped the velvet bag on the floor and they were fighting over it. "Bunch of hooligans," Isabel muttered, taking the pouch and pretending to scold them. "I can just see one of you choking on the string."

Jeremy laughed. "Can I make another crazy suggestion?"

"On top of marriage?"

"Yes. Let's keep the kittens. And Cat. Let's not give them up for adoption."

Isabel could hardly believe the words that had

just come from Jeremy's mouth, which was saying a lot given that he'd just proposed. "But you don't really like cats."

"Like a lot of things, you managed to show me what I was missing out on."

"It'll be a ton of work. Four cats running around here."

Jeremy shrugged and pulled her closer. "So? I have spent years walking around this big house, hardly using it or enjoying it for that matter. And then I met you and the whole place sprang back to life. I don't want to hold back on that. So we have four cats and a baby. Bring it on."

Isabel smiled harder than she'd ever smiled, even more than she had while watching her brother say "I do" mere hours ago. "Oh, you know what I just realized? If I change my name to Isabel Blackwell-Sharp after we get married, you can still keep the firm's name as Sharp and Sharp."

"First off, I'm not doing the same thing to you that my dad did to me. We will change the firm's name to whatever you want it to be. To whatever you want your last name to be."

She then realized what a pushover she was being. "You've got me into way too much of a charitable mood, Sharp. I should be negotiating with you, not offering concessions from the word go."

"I don't want to talk work, Isabel." He threaded his fingers through her hair, then rubbed his thumb along her lower lip. "I don't want to talk about who we know or what we do."

Isabel smiled at the echo of the magical night they'd met, when she'd dared to take a chance on Jeremy. How lucky was she that he ended up being the one? "Yeah? Then what do you want to talk about?"

"How do you feel about good views? Because there's a spectacular one in our bedroom."

* * * * *

Don't miss the other three stories
in Karen Booth's miniseries,
The Eden Empire:

A Bet with Benefits
A Cinderella Seduction
A Christmas Temptation

COMING NEXT MONTH FROM

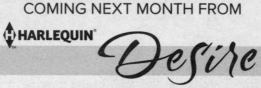

HARLEQUIN *Desire*

Available December 3, 2019

#2701 DUTY OR DESIRE
The Westmoreland Legacy • by Brenda Jackson
Becoming guardian of his young niece is tough for Westmoreland neighbor
Pete Higgins. But Myra Hollister, the irresistible new nanny with a dangerous
past, pushes him to the brink. Will desire for the nanny distract him from duty to
his niece?

#2702 TEMPTING THE TEXAN
Texas Cattleman's Club: Inheritance • by Maureen Child
When a family tragedy calls rancher Kellan Blackwood home to Royal, Texas,
he's reunited with the woman he left behind, Irina Romanov. Can the secrets
that drove them apart in the first place bring them back together?

#2703 THE RIVAL
Dynasties: Mesa Falls • by Joanne Rock
Media mogul Devon Salazar is suspicious of the seductive new tour guide at
Mesa Falls Ranch. Sure enough, Regina Flores wants to take him down after
his father destroyed her family. But attraction to her target might take her
down first...

#2704 RED CARPET REDEMPTION
The Stewart Heirs • by Yahrah St. John
Dane Stewart is a Hollywood heartthrob with a devilish reputation. When a
sperm bank mishap reveals he has a secret child with the beautiful but guarded
Iris Turner, their intense chemistry surprises them both. Can this made-for-the-
movies romance last?

#2705 ONE NIGHT TO RISK IT ALL
One Night • by Katherine Garbera
After a night of passion, Inigo Velasquez learns that socialite Marielle Bisset is
the woman who ruined his sister's marriage. A staged seduction to avenge his
sister might quell his moral outrage... But will it quench his desire for Marielle?

#2706 TWIN SCANDALS
The Pearl House • by Fiona Brand
Seeking payback against the man who dumped her, Sophie Messena switches
places with her twin on a business trip with billionaire Ben Sabin. When they are
stranded by a storm, their attraction surges. But will past scandals threaten their
chance at a future?

Get 4 FREE REWARDS!

We'll send you 2 FREE Books plus 2 FREE Mystery Gifts.

Harlequin® Desire books feature heroes who have it all: wealth, status, incredible good looks... everything but the right woman.

FREE
Value Over
$20

SPECIAL EXCERPT FROM

HQN™

New York Times *bestselling author Brenda Jackson welcomes you to Catalina Cove, where even the biggest heartbreaks can be healed...*

Read on for a sneak peek at
Finding Home Again...

A flash of pink moving around in his house made Kaegan frown when he recalled just who'd worn that particular color tonight. He glanced back at Sasha. "Tell Farley that I hope he starts feeling better. Good night." Without waiting for Sasha's response, he quickly walked off, heading inside his home.

He heard a noise coming from the kitchen. Moving quickly, he walked in to find Bryce Witherspoon on a ladder putting something in one of the cabinets. Anger, to a degree he hadn't felt in a long time, consumed him. Standing there in his kitchen on that ladder was the one and only woman he'd ever loved. The one woman he would risk his life for, and he recalled doing so once. She was the only woman who'd had his heart from the time they were in grade school. The only one he'd ever wanted to marry, have his babies. The only one who...

He realized he'd been standing there recalling things he preferred not remembering. What he should be remembering was that she was the woman who'd broken his heart. "What the hell are you doing in here, Bryce?"

His loud, booming voice startled her. She jerked around, lost her balance and came tumbling off the ladder. He rushed over and caught her in his arms before she could hit the floor. His chest tightened and his nerves, and a few other parts of his anatomy, kicked in the moment his hands and arms touched the body he used to know as well as his own. A body he'd introduced to passion. A body he'd—

"Put me down, Kaegan Chambray!"

He started to drop her, just for the hell of it. She was such a damn ingrate. "Next time I'll just let you fall on your ass," he snapped, placing her on her feet and trying not to notice how beautiful she was. Her eyes were a cross of hazel and moss green, and were adorned by long eyelashes. She had high cheekbones and shoulder-length curly brown hair. Her skin was a gorgeous honey brown and her lips, although at the moment curved in a frown, had always been one of her most noticeable traits.

PHBJEXP1119

"Let go of my hand, Kaegan!"

Her sharp tone made him realize he'd been standing there staring at her. He fought to regain his senses. "What are you doing, going through my cabinets?"

She rounded on him, tossing all that beautiful hair out of her face. "I was on that ladder putting your spices back in the cabinets."

He crossed his arms over his chest. "Why?"

"Because I was helping you tidy up after the party by putting things away."

She had to be kidding. "I don't need your help."

"Fine! I'll leave, then. You can take Vashti home."

Take Vashti home? What the hell was she talking about? He was about to ask when Vashti burst into the kitchen. "What in the world is going on? I heard the two of you yelling and screaming all the way in the bathroom."

Kaegan turned to Vashti. "What is she talking about, me taking you home? Where's Sawyer?"

"He got a call and had to leave. I asked Bryce to drop me off at home. I also asked her to assist me in helping you straighten up before we left."

"I don't need help."

Bryce rounded on him. "Why don't you tell her what you told me? Namely, that you don't need *my* help."

He had no problem doing that. Glancing back at Vashti, he said. "I don't need Bryce's help. Nor do I want it."

Bryce looked at Vashti. "I'm leaving. You either come with me now or he can take you home."

Vashti looked from one to the other and then threw up her hands in frustration. "I'm leaving with you, Bryce. I'll be out to the car in a minute."

When Bryce walked out of the kitchen, Kaegan turned to Vashti. "You had no right asking her to stay here after the party to do anything, Vashti. I don't want her here. The only reason I even invited her is because of you."

Kaegan had seen fire in Vashti's eyes before, but it had never been directed at him. Now it was. She crossed the room and he had a mind to take a step back, but he didn't. "I'm sick and tired of you acting like an ass where Bryce is concerned, Kaegan. When will you wake up and realize what you accused her of all those years ago is not true?"

He glared at her. "Oh? Is that what she told you? News flash—you weren't there, Vashti, and I know what I saw."

"Do you?"

"Yes. So, you can believe the lie she's telling you all you want, but I know what I saw that night."

Vashti drew in a deep breath. "Do you? Or do you only know what you think you saw?"

Then without saying anything else, she turned and walked out of the kitchen.

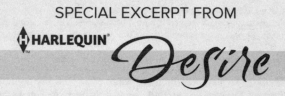
"That's it, Peterson Higgins, no more. You've had three servings already," Myra said, laughing, as she guarded the pan of peach cobbler on the counter.

He stood in front of her, grinning from ear to ear. "You should not have baked it so well. It was delicious."

"Thanks, but flattery won't get you any more peach cobbler tonight. You've had your limit."

He crossed his arms over his chest. "I could have you arrested, you know."

Crossing her arms over her own chest, she tilted her chin and couldn't stop grinning. "On what charge?"

The charge that immediately came to Pete's mind was that she was so darn beautiful. Irresistible. But he figured that was something he could not say.

She snapped her fingers in front of his face to reclaim his attention. "If you have to think that hard about a charge, then that means there isn't one."

"Oh, you'll be surprised what all I can do, Myra."

She tilted her head to the side as if to look at him better. "Do tell, Pete."

Her words—those three little words—made a full-blown attack on his senses. He drew in a shaky breath, then touched her chin. She blinked, as if startled by his touch. "How about 'do show,' Myra?"

Pete watched the way the lump formed in her throat and detected her shift in breathing. He could even hear the pounding of her heart. Damn, she smelled good, and she looked good, too. Always did.

"I'm not sure what 'do show' means," she said in a voice that was as shaky as his had been.

He tilted her chin up to gaze into her eyes, as well as to study the shape of her exquisite lips. "Then let me demonstrate, Ms. Hollister," he said, lowering his mouth to hers.

The moment he swept his tongue inside her mouth and tasted her, he was a goner. It took every ounce of strength he had to keep the kiss gentle when he wanted to devour her mouth with a hunger he felt all the way in his bones. A part of him wanted to take the kiss deeper, but then another part wanted to savor her taste. Honestly, either worked for him as long as she felt the passion between them.

He had wanted her from the moment he'd set eyes on her, but he'd fought the desire. He could no longer do that. He was a man known to forego his own needs and desires, but tonight he couldn't.

Whispering close to her ear, he said, "Peach cobbler isn't the only thing I could become addicted to, Myra."

Will their first kiss distract him from his duty?

Find out in
Duty or Desire
by New York Times *bestselling author Brenda Jackson.*

Available December 2019 wherever
Harlequin® Desire books and ebooks are sold.

Harlequin.com